PRAISE FOR CHAD ZUNKER

Family Money

"The action barrels along to a shocking conclusion . . . Zunker knows how to keep the reader hooked."

—*Publishers Weekly*

An Equal Justice

Harper Lee Prize for Legal Fiction Finalist

"A deftly crafted legal thriller of a novel by an author with a genuine knack for a reader-engaging narrative storytelling style."

—*Midwest Book Review*

"A gripping thriller with a heart, *An Equal Justice* hits the ground running . . . The chapters flew by, with surprises aplenty and taut writing. A highly recommended read that introduces a lawyer with legs."

—Crime Thriller Hound

"In *An Equal Justice*, author Chad Zunker crafts a riveting legal thriller . . . *An Equal Justice* not only plunges readers into murder and conspiracy involving wealthy power players but also immerses us in the crisis of homelessness in our country."

—*The Big Thrill*

"A thriller with a message. A pleasure to read. Twists I didn't see coming. I read it in one sitting."

—Robert Dugoni, #1 Amazon bestselling author of *My Sister's Grave*

"Taut, suspenseful, and action packed with a hero you can root for, Zunker has hit it out of the park with this one."

—Victor Methos, bestselling author of *The Neon Lawyer*

An Unequal Defense

"In Zunker's solid sequel to 2019's *An Equal Justice*, Zunker . . . sustains a disciplined focus on plot and character. John Grisham fans will appreciate this familiar but effective tale."

—*Publishers Weekly*

Runaway Justice

"[In the] engrossing third mystery featuring attorney David Adams . . . Zunker gives heart and hope to his characters. There are no lulls in this satisfying story of a young runaway in trouble."

—*Publishers Weekly*

IN HIS WAKE

ALSO BY CHAD ZUNKER

Not Our Daughter

The Wife You Know

All He Has Left

Family Money

David Adams Series

An Equal Justice

An Unequal Defense

Runaway Justice

Sam Callahan Series

The Tracker

Shadow Shepherd

Hunt the Lion

IN HIS WAKE

CHAD ZUNKER

This is a work of fiction. Names, characters, organizations, places, events, and incidents are either products of the author's imagination or are used fictitiously. Otherwise, any resemblance to actual persons, living or dead, is purely coincidental.

Published by Thomas & Mercer, Seattle

www.apub.com

EU product safety contact:
Amazon Media EU S. à r.l.
38, avenue John F. Kennedy, L-1855 Luxembourg
amazonpublishing-gpsr@amazon.com

ISBN-13: 9781662534577 (paperback)
ISBN-13: 9781662529917 (digital)

Cover design by Logan Matthews
Cover image: © gabriel-alenius / Unsplash; © Henry Horenstein, © Nora Carol Photography / Getty

Printed in the United States of America

To Wade and Monty, the best brothers

ONE

They found him in Costa Rica.

They followed him in the shadows for three days. He'd lost some serious weight, probably more than fifty pounds, but gained a golden tan. Gone was the pale skin and girth they'd observed in the profile pictures. Gone were the puffy cheeks and bloodshot eyes, the look of a man who spent every day in a plush high-rise office working mind-numbing hours. The hair was nearly the same, though, peppered gray and trimmed up short to the scalp.

The hair was a mistake. He should have completely changed it.

Bryson Carter led the field operation. He was a twenty-year CIA man who'd run covert missions all over the globe before going private and joining the secretive security group in DC. He had a team of five working with him. All former agents like him who were ready to get paid well for their skill sets.

The man spent most days on the beach. Blue-jean cutoffs, no shirt, sandals, still a slight belly—probably from his clear affection for Imperial, Costa Ricans' favorite local beer. A gray beard now covered his chin. In his past life, he was clean-shaven and ready for court. The chin had been altered. They were sure of that. Rounded off at the edges. Maybe the cheekbones, too. The face was much tighter, and not just from the rapid weight loss. He looked ten years younger. He'd hired a skilled professional. That was smart. They were interviewing local plastic surgeons, but he could have had it done anywhere. They sent digital surveillance images back to the home office in DC on the first day. Their identification software gave them a 92 percent affirmative match.

He wore his sixty-two years well. Lean arms and strong shoulders. He lived alone on a thirty-two-foot sailboat that he worked on most days. A real beach bum. The only people he regularly interacted with were the locals in a dumpy bar called Jacko's Paradise. They asked around. Jacko didn't know much about him, said he'd been coming into the bar for about two months, called himself Red, and mostly kept to himself. Always paid in cash. The two men had talked about baseball and boats but not much else.

There was nothing inside the sailboat that identified him. No wallet with a driver's license, no credit cards, no passport, no used airline tickets, no prescription medicine, no old magazines with subscription labels, and no official boat records. He clearly didn't want to be known. In their three days of monitoring him, they had not seen one other person climb aboard his sailboat. They'd been inside already, on the first day. There were no hidden compartments on the boat. No safes under the bed or in the back of a tiny closet. No secret files. Nothing. They'd searched every corner without leaving a trace of their presence.

He paid for everything in cash. They found a thick envelope with about $5,000 worth of colón, Costa Rican currency, tucked beneath the worn mattress. He had more money elsewhere. Millions more, if their client file was correct. An anonymous Cayman account? A safe-deposit box? A secret locker?

They were digging. They would find it.

He never used a cell phone. They'd yet to see him use any phone. He owned a weathered stack of old Louis L'Amour Westerns. There was no TV in the sailboat. No internet. There was an old iPod with a few albums on it. Merle Haggard. Johnny Cash. Hank Williams. Other country singers they didn't recognize. The music account was inactive. The iPod had, at one time, been registered to a college student out of Miami. They had people there who had spoken directly to the kid. The student said someone had paid him $200 cash for the device at a bus stop four months ago and then had him download music. They felt the student was telling the truth.

They found him. But nothing else yet that connected him to his crime. The clock was ticking. They could not observe him forever.

Near the end of the third day, they followed him through the busy local market. It was hot, crowded, and noisy. They watched as he purchased bread and fruit and looked so at ease among the locals. They were surprised at his casual demeanor. He never looked nervous. He rarely checked over his shoulder, searching for eyes that might be watching him. They thought this was unusual for someone in his position. He was not one of them, a former spy or military specialist trained in evasion tactics. On the surface, he was not someone who could easily set up a new life in another country. He was only trained in the law. A paper pusher. A simple corporate attorney on the run. A former law partner who'd scammed millions from the wrong men. And who'd almost gotten away with it.

Hidden in the shadow of an alley, ten feet away, one of them said his name, just loud enough to be heard over the clatter of the busy outdoor marketplace. "Dawson!" They watched. He flinched, turned, just slightly but enough to reassure them. His eyes went back to the guava in his hand. He then swiftly paid for his items and left the market.

They would take him quickly. An unmarked van was waiting around the corner. They'd already secured a tiny cabin deep in the jungle. A place where a man could scream at the top of his lungs for countless hours and no one would hear him. They would get the answers they wanted. They always did. They were professionals who could be very persuasive. No one had lasted more than a week.

They followed him down the dirt road to the beach. They'd been ready for him to run. Instead, he walked at a steady pace, kept his eyes ahead, and looked calm. But he didn't know his elaborate plan had slowly come unraveled. He didn't know he'd been discovered back in the States. He was unaware they'd been searching for him for the past month. And now he'd been found.

The dead man had come back to life.

TWO

The familiar brown UPS truck was stolen three states away.

It was given new plates and untethered from company tracking devices.

His client's men had left it for him in a parking lot around the corner from his Austin hotel. The key was sitting in a crack in the tread on the back tire. He would leave the vehicle in a junkyard outside the city, where they were instructed to destroy it. There could be no traces. His name was Yusuf Demir. But most in his secretive world called him the Caracal. A name derived from a medium-size wildcat found in the Middle East and Africa, and known to be highly difficult to observe. It was an accurate description. He'd been trained in the Bordo Bereliler—considered the elite unit of the Turkish military—before becoming one of the most lethal assassins in the world.

He'd never worked in the United States. Until today.

He parked the truck in an alley behind the pristine thirty-three-story Frost Bank Tower in the heart of downtown and checked his watch. Ten fifteen in the evening. If everything was still on schedule, he had exactly twenty-two minutes to get in position. He got out of the truck and adjusted his custom-fit brown UPS uniform. No detail of this operation could be overlooked. He circled to the back of the truck, opened the door, and pulled out a heavy-duty dolly. He then loaded it up with several large UPS-marked boxes.

After shutting the truck door, he wheeled the dolly down the alley toward the underground delivery entrance to the high-rise office building. He could see the old security guard through a window just inside the check-in door. Demir plucked a key card from his front shirt pocket and held it up to the security scanner. The light on the scanner went from red to green, and the secured door clicked open. He grinned, relieved. He didn't want to have to unnecessarily kill a security guard. That would only complicate things. The guard placed a clipboard in front of him as he stepped up to the counter.

"How're you doing tonight?" Demir asked.

His English was perfect. He'd hired a private tutor more than a decade ago. It had to be perfect for him to operate all over the globe.

"Hanging in there," the guard said, barely looking up.

Demir glanced behind the guard and over to the corner of the booth. Security camera. Didn't matter. He wore a black knit cap, glasses, and a fake beard. He thought he could hear a football game coming from a cell phone hidden beneath the counter. Americans loved their football. He'd watched their beloved Super Bowl once. It had bored him. He preferred soccer (what the Americans called it). Demir filled out the appropriate information on the clipboard, grabbed the dolly, and hauled it around a corner to a pair of service elevators. He was inside a few seconds later and traveling alone up to the top floor of the building.

He checked his watch again. Right on time. When the elevator arrived, he quickly got off. A financial consulting firm called Atlantis leased the entire top floor. But Demir wasn't visiting the company. Instead, he found a janitor's closet in the hallway around the corner from the firm's glass doors and pushed the dolly inside. He then grabbed a slender box from the dolly that was long enough to hold a telescope lens. But that was not what was inside the container. He shut the closet, stepped around a corner, and approached a door leading to the stairwell.

With the box tucked in his right arm, he swiftly ascended the stairs. Once he reached the next level—one that was only for maintenance and mechanical work—Demir located a steel ladder attached to a wall that led to the building's rooftop.

He climbed up with the box in tow, pushed through a metal door above, and was staring down at the Austin skyline a moment later. He walked a full circle to take in the view in each direction. To the north, the well-lit, massive pink granite of the Texas State Capitol building. To the south, the Colorado River, hugged on both sides by walking trails. He'd never been to the city. He'd heard the music scene was superb. Maybe he'd find out for himself on another trip. Demir maneuvered around the rooftop and made his way to the side facing southeast. He found a position between two jagged-glass panels, set the box down, and tore it open. Inside, he pulled out a hard black case. After popping it open, Demir stared down at the pieces of his impressive sniper rifle.

He checked his watch. He was three minutes ahead of schedule.

As he had a thousand times before, he went through his routine of meticulously putting the rifle together and checking all the calibrations. Satisfied, he set the gun's bipod on top of the concrete wall and allowed the long rifle barrel to peek out over the ledge. Demir removed his fake glasses and placed his sharp eye to the custom-built scope. He adjusted the rifle through several skyscrapers and found his target. The front of the Four Seasons Hotel was 812 meters away. Through the powerful scope, it seemed more like five feet. He'd hit targets from four times the distance. He could see the wrinkles on the forehead of a black-haired bellman standing just outside the glass doors. It was a cool October evening. Thankfully, there was very little wind tonight. Three miles per hour out of the northeast. It was consistent and not swirling. Near-ideal conditions. The wind was critical for success and was part of his $40 million contract. If there was too much wind, he could walk away and keep $1 million just for showing up. But he refused to leave the other $39 million on the table.

Demir felt the tiny disposable cell phone vibrate in his pocket. It was a phone left for him inside the glove box of the UPS truck, only for this mission. Like everything else, it would be destroyed shortly.

He reached down, pulled it out, read the text message.

Two minutes. All is set.

He repositioned himself, eye to scope, and took a few deep breaths. He began focusing on members of the intense security detail surrounding the luxury hotel. Over two dozen men in dark suits, out on sidewalks, steps, parking lots—undoubtedly a mix of FBI and Secret Service. Demir quickly counted at least another eight men with rifles paired with spotters with binoculars on top of surrounding buildings. Secret Service sniper teams. He was certain he was outside their protective bubble.

A string of black Suburbans suddenly turned off the street and entered the hotel's circular drive. Four of them in a row. His info told him vehicle number three held his target. The Suburbans began parking directly in front of the hotel. Men in dark suits jumped out on all sides, even more men scrambling into protective positions. A group of them huddled around the doors of the third vehicle, a wall of human bodies, men willing to lay down their lives for their country. Demir would only have a split second to engage. There was zero room for error.

He reached up and pressed a button on a tiny black box the size of a small battery that was connected to the powerful scope. The entire incident would be recorded. Thanks to technology, the world would soon get to watch his achievement in high-definition detail. This was also part of his contract.

Two men exited the vehicle first.

His finger flinched ever so slightly on the trigger upon spotting the second man. But he stopped. Not yet. Not him.

Then a third man appeared. Stood straight. Glanced to his left. It was him.

Demir squeezed the trigger. The rifle engaged. The bullet cut perfectly through the air. The Caracal didn't blink. He didn't move. He barely breathed. Had he calculated precisely? He then saw the familiar spray of blood and tissue explode from his target's head. And the wonderful chaos that immediately followed.

A perfect $40 million kill shot.

THREE

Dean Dawson was sitting in his reporter's cubicle at the Austin headquarters of *TexasNow*, an online investigative news outlet, struggling to find the right words for a possible feature story, when he heard a sudden ruckus coming from around the corner in what they all called the bullpen. What the hell had just happened? He jumped from his chair and hurried down a hallway to a lounge area with a wall of TVs showing every major cable news channel. A small group of reporters and editors were staring wide-eyed at the TVs. Like him, most of the team worked late, hoping to put something worthwhile on cell phone screens by the time their readers rolled out of bed the next morning. But Dean knew immediately that no one was going to be reading their stories in a few hours. Not when every TV channel was currently flashing a similar bold and shocking headline.

Carson Assassinated

Dean cursed, moved closer to the TVs. No way. Was this real? He connected eyes with another reporter, a guy named Manny, who wore the same slack-jawed look. Senator Carson had flown into Austin earlier in the afternoon to attend a high-dollar fundraiser at a tech billionaire's lakeside mansion. The country was only two weeks from Election Day.

Every movement the two candidates made on the trail these days was under scrutiny. Dean's eyes bounced from screen to screen. The news channels were all showing clips from the same chaotic scene around the front of what he clearly recognized as the Four Seasons. The hotel was only five blocks from their fourth-floor downtown office inside the historic Scarborough Building.

"You believe this?" a steady voice said behind him.

Dean turned to see his editor, Harvey Kingsley, standing next to him. Harvey was mid-sixties, slender, with perfectly sculpted silver hair. He still wore a dress shirt and tie every day to the office, even though his twentysomething subordinates, like Dean, dressed mostly in jeans, T-shirts, and sneakers. His editor was old-school like that. He'd spent decades at legacy papers in New York and Boston before settling down in Austin several years back to be near his grandchildren.

"Yes and no!" Dean exclaimed, running a hand through his wavy brown hair. "I guess I shouldn't be too surprised. We live in a crazy world right now. But still . . . damn."

"Yeah. I figured someone would eventually pull off an assassination of this magnitude. Just never expected it to happen in our own backyard."

"This is so big, Harvey."

"First assassination like this since Bobby Kennedy."

"Incredible. What do you think? Foreign? Domestic?"

Harvey shrugged. "Who the hell knows? Could be a lone gunman. The bigger question for us right now is, how do we cover it? You talk to your brother yet?"

"No. He's probably there already."

"Go find out. See what you can pull together."

"Yes, sir. I'm on it."

Dean grabbed his brown leather jacket, took the elevator to the ground floor, and hustled the five blocks down Congress Avenue toward East

Cesar Chavez Street. The Four Seasons sat on the banks of the Colorado River, surrounded by several other luxury hotels and high-rise office buildings. He could hear the chaos long before he ever arrived. When he turned the final corner, he was met with a swarm of police and medical vehicles, their red and blue lights flickering off adjacent buildings like a laser light show. An already growing crowd of onlookers was being held back by uniformed officers. Again, Dean shook his head. It felt surreal to be standing this close to such a historical event.

He pushed his way through the crowd and got as close as he could before being stopped near the hotel property premises by the strong hand of a barrel-chested police officer. Dean spotted a row of black Suburbans all parked directly outside the front of the hotel. He'd seen this same shot on TV. Dozens of security personnel were scrambling about all over the place. He presumed Secret Service. Glancing to his left, he took in the TV news channels' cameras all aimed in the same direction. Several prominent national reporters who were covering the campaign stood in front of bright lights with microphones in their hands.

Dean turned back to the crime scene. He counted a dozen men and women wearing the same familiar dark-blue jackets with the yellow "FBI" imprinted on the back. He was searching for one face in particular and located him standing just behind the last black Suburban, huddled with two other FBI agents.

"Eric!" Dean called out loud enough to be heard over the crowd.

His brother turned, squinted. Dean waved his arms to get his attention. Spotting him, Eric walked in his direction. At thirty-two, his brother was four years older and a couple of inches taller. Eric had thrown the javelin in college and still looked like he could give it a good heave today. He used to regularly kick Dean's ass when they'd wrestled as kids. But then Dean hit the weights as part of the high school football team and was eventually able to hold his own. Eric had basically raised him and his youngest brother, Ben, after their father had abandoned them when they were young. Their mom had been a disaster after her divorce from their father and never really recovered. Alcoholism had eventually led to her death last year. While Dean had resented his father for many reasons over the years—a near lifetime of lies and broken promises—his mother's demise last October was at the top of the list.

Eric instructed the police officer to allow Dean through.

"I thought you might be here," Dean said.

Eric blew air out heavily. "Yeah, well, my team was providing backup security."

Eric was a special agent in charge of Austin's FBI office. He'd spent seven years in DC before requesting the assignment change ten months ago so that his wife, Tina, could be closer to her ailing mother. Although Dean had been glad to have his big brother around again, Eric regularly complained about how boring the work was here in Texas compared to the fast-paced energy of the nation's capital.

But that had dramatically changed tonight.

"What the hell happened?" Dean asked.

"You asking as my brother or as a reporter?"

"Can it be both?"

"No."

"Okay, just your brother. For now."

Eric's eyes narrowed to slits.

"I swear," Dean reassured him.

Eric ran a hand over his shaved head. Unlike Dean, who had a full head of thick hair, Eric had gone prematurely bald. So he'd chosen the Mr. Clean route a few years ago.

"Sniper shot," Eric revealed. "Had to be from a good distance away, too, because Secret Service had sniper units in the immediate vicinity. We're going building to building. But we're not making fast enough progress. We're a smaller office. San Antonio has thirty more agents en route to me right now."

"Anyone else get hit?"

Eric grimaced. "Yeah, one of my guys. Nelson. Bullet went straight through Carson and struck him square in the neck. He's about to go into emergency surgery. Doesn't look good. Nelson has a brand-new baby at home. It's awful, bro."

"I'm sorry to hear that. Anything I can do to help?"

"Don't publish stupid conspiracy theories that make my job even harder."

"You know I don't do that kind of thing."

Eric held up his buzzing phone and cursed.

"Tina?" Dean queried.

"Worse. The director. I gotta go, man."

"Hang in there. I'll call you later."

"All right."

Dean watched as Eric returned to the crime scene. He felt sorry for his brother, who would likely have to stand in front of TV cameras shortly and explain how this had happened in his city and on his watch. Eric was already going through a rough patch, having just recently separated from Tina. His brother had two young, confused boys at home. Dean had spent extra time with his nephews over the past couple of weeks, playing basketball, going for ice cream, and taking them to the latest superhero movies. Just trying to give the boys a healthy distraction away from their parents' current marital troubles.

Dean felt his own phone vibrate in his pocket and pulled it out. His eyes narrowed. He was shocked to see a message from his ex-girlfriend April North. They hadn't texted or spoken since she'd broken up with him nearly a year ago. That still stung, even though it had been his fault. But more surprising was the message she'd just sent him.

I need to see you right away.

There was no introductory *Hey, how are you?* message. She got right to the point. But as an attorney, April had always been succinct with her words. She used to tease him about overwriting his stories. He had to remind her there was still art in journalism that was mostly absent in her boring legal briefs.

Why did she want to see him?

He texted a response: Hey. What's going on?

I can't say over the phone.

Okay. Coffee tomorrow?

No, it must be tonight.

His brow bunched. Had she not seen the news?

Tonight is crazy. Turn on the TV.

Please, Dean. Tonight.

He stared at her desperately worded plea. It was unlike her. April had always been fiercely independent and never liked to admit she needed help. She hadn't even let him carry the heavy grocery bags when they were dating. She'd always wanted to prove she was just as strong as he was. So what was the deal here?

Okay, where?

Our usual spot. Twenty minutes.

FOUR

Their usual spot was the Driskill Bar, off Austin's popular Sixth Street near the heart of the entertainment district. The laid-back bar was on the second level of the famous Driskill hotel, where many US presidents had stayed over the years. Everything was rich and mahogany, with rustic leather couches and cowhide barstools. Because it was easy walking distance from both of their offices, they would often slip away to the Driskill for drinks in a quiet atmosphere when they were together. The bar was nearly empty tonight. A couple of older gentlemen wearing business suits sat in a booth in the corner, and two women who looked like they could be mother and daughter were enjoying cocktails and sharing laughs.

April was already waiting for him at the end of the bar. At twenty-six, April had graduated near the top of her law school class at the University of Virginia two years ago before taking a job at the powerhouse corporate law firm Michaels & Peterson. Dean had followed her social media postings the past year. Which was probably stupid. She'd appeared to have easily moved on from him. That was painful enough, but seeing her up close was worse. She looked as breathtaking as ever, with her shoulder-length brown hair, fit figure, and mesmerizing hazel eyes. She was dressed in black slacks, a white silk blouse, and black heels, which told him she'd walked straight over from her twenty-second-floor office.

Dean sidled up onto the barstool next to her. He immediately smelled her familiar fragrance, and it unexpectedly rattled him. For a moment, he wondered if it was a mistake for him to come. He was still in love with her. Time had healed nothing.

"Hey," he said.

"Hey back," she replied. "You look good, Dean."

"You look great," he countered, probably with too much enthusiasm.

She gave him a quick grin. One with her cute dimples. The kind she'd always give him right before they kissed. He felt another heart flutter. Damn. She slid a glass of bourbon she'd ordered in advance in front of him and then took a sip from her own. This was also their usual. He'd always loved that April would drink whiskey with him. She'd do a lot of things other girls he'd dated normally wouldn't. Watch college football all day on Saturdays. Play golf. Shoot pool. She grew up with two older sports-loving brothers, her father was a football coach, and she'd played a variety of high school athletics. Volleyball. Basketball. Track. So it was in her blood. She was also so dang competitive. One-on-one basketball between them would sometimes get physical when she was losing. The girl had a quick temper and sharp elbows. She'd even thrown the ball at his head once, which made him laugh but only pissed her off even more.

"Are you okay?" he asked. "Your text was a surprise, to say the least."

"I'm not sure," she admitted.

"What's wrong, April? I mean, I hear nothing from you for a year. And then tonight, of all nights, you demand to see me?"

"You'll understand in a moment."

She grabbed her phone from her small black purse, pulled something up on the screen, and then set the device down in front of him. He picked it up. On the screen was a photo of a text message exchange. The name at the top said *Rainer*. The other person on the text exchange was unidentified. He quickly read through it.

Rainer: Dawson still hasn't broken. He's a tough SOB.

Always has been. I've known him twenty years.

Rainer: How would you like to proceed?

Is our friend already here?

Rainer: Yes. He will perform if money hits his account.

We're out of time. Scorpion green-lights. Money is being wired.

Rainer: Copy that. In 24 hours, Carson should no longer be a problem.

Dean's eyes widened. He reread the entire text exchange, just to make sure his vision wasn't betraying him. *Dawson still hasn't broken. Carson should no longer be a problem.* What the hell?

He looked over at April. "Where did you get this?"

"My boss's phone. Late last night."

"Your boss is still Edward Sullivan, the managing partner?"

"Yes."

"But . . . how did you—"

"My trial team was working in a conference room. Sullivan set his cell phone down on the table in front of me to grab a call on the firm's landline behind us. His phone was left wide open. I couldn't help but glance down. This is what was on the screen. It was the mention of the name 'Dawson' that initially grabbed me last night. I pretended to be sending a text on my own phone and snapped this photo without him noticing. At least, I thought. I'm not so sure now."

"Who is Rainer?"

"I don't know. I'm not familiar with the name."

Dean's mind was suddenly spinning. He read the first line of the text exchange again. *Dawson still hasn't broken. He's a tough SOB.*

"Is there another Dawson at your firm?" he asked.

She shook her head.

"A client?"

"No. At least, I can't find one. I thought of sending this to you last night. But I hadn't decided what to do with it until everything blew up on the news this evening."

"This doesn't make any sense, April."

"I'm as baffled as you."

Dean grabbed his glass of bourbon off the bar counter and finally took a sip. Jerry Dawson was Dean's father. He'd been a longtime partner with Sullivan at the law firm of Michaels & Peterson before dying in a solo boating accident on Austin's Lake Travis four months ago. Based off the number of empty liquor bottles they'd found on the boat, police suspected he'd drunkenly fallen over and drowned. However, they never recovered his body.

While he held animosity toward his father for many things over the years, meeting April was not one of them. Dean had accepted tickets from his father to a University of Texas football game two years ago, where the law firm leased a private suite. Dean had met April there, who was then a first-year associate with the firm. They'd hit it off immediately, talking and flirting the entire game instead of paying any attention to what was happening on the field.

"My father is dead," Dean said, stating the obvious.

"Yeah, I know. I was at the funeral."

"Right," he acknowledged.

"You were not," she reminded him.

Dean had been so angry about how his father had died, especially after they'd just started to rebuild their broken relationship, that he'd chosen not to attend. His absence had made his younger brother, Ben, furious. Ben still wasn't speaking to him because of it. His little brother had always been more forgiving than Dean. But then, he'd been only three years old when their father had left. He hadn't been old enough to experience the devastating pain of it all. He couldn't remember their mom barely coming out of her bedroom for nearly two months. And when she did, she was only going out to buy more alcohol. Those were dark days that had left deep scars.

"Your father aside, what do you make of the rest of the text?"

Dean blew air out forcefully. "It reads like a nuclear bomb, to be honest. It would be a hell of a coincidence if they weren't talking about tonight's assassination."

"Yeah, and that's terrifying."

"Does your firm have a client connected to Senator Carson?"

"We represent all kinds of corporations and lobbying firms who are intricately involved in DC politics. The list is endless."

"The text says *Scorpion green-lights.*"

"Another mystery. No clue. I've been searching through client files the past hour but have come up with nothing related to a 'Scorpion' so far. I'm really scared, Dean. Although I was careful last night, I think my boss might have noticed me taking this photo. When he finished his call, he snagged his phone and eyeballed me the rest of the evening. And then he unexpectedly took me off his trial team this morning."

"He give you a reason?"

"Nope. But he's Edward Sullivan. He doesn't have to give reasons."

"This is absolutely shocking. On all fronts."

Dean was having difficulty processing all this. A man who would've likely been elected president next month had been assassinated while in Austin. Four blocks away from where he'd been sitting at his newsroom desk. That was stunning enough. But now both his father and former girlfriend were somehow connected? Could his dad still be alive? The text certainly implied it. That crazy thought nearly made his head split open.

"What do you think we should do?" April asked.

"Probably go to the feds. Maybe talk to my brother."

"I can't do that, Dean. You think it's a smart career move for me to turn in my boss over something that's unconfirmed? I know this looks bad, but we really don't know what this is all about. Not to mention I could be unwittingly in violation of attorney-client privilege and potentially get disbarred."

"I didn't think about that."

"Do you think your father is still alive?"

"I don't know what to think right now."

"Well, this is why I came to you. I can't trust anyone else."

Dean had to admit it felt good to hear her say that, even after a year apart. He took full blame for why things had ended between them. His mother's diagnosis and quick death last year had pushed him into a dark hole. His mom had finally gotten sober. She was making a new life for herself. A life that wasn't dominated by her drinking. She had started teaching again. She'd gotten involved with a church. She'd even started dating a nice older man. She was happy. And then the liver cancer came out of nowhere and crushed everything. It took her swiftly. Dean had been so angry. At God. At his father. At the world. At himself for not being able to somehow help her get sober sooner, before any cancer had taken root. Because of this, he shut out everyone, including April. By the time he'd recovered, she was already dating someone new.

"Have you told anyone else about this?" he asked.

"No, just you."

"What about Josh?"

Josh Manefield was his replacement. An attorney with another corporate firm. A guy who looked like he belonged on the cover of *GQ*. Tall, dark, and handsome. The full trifecta. Although Dean had never met him, he still hated him.

"I broke up with Josh a few months ago," April revealed.

"Oh, sorry to hear that."

Dean tried to conceal just how pleased he was to hear that. She didn't say "we" broke up a few months ago. She said she broke up with him. Was that intentional? He swallowed, forced back the thought. Now was certainly not the time to entertain it. April was in trouble here. He had to focus on that. He asked April to text him the message exchange between her boss and Rainer.

"Okay, let me begin digging into this."

"What should I do?"

"Nothing," Dean insisted, eyes narrow. "If we believe this is what we think, April, you could be in danger. You need to stay the hell away from this. You should probably hide out until we figure this all out."

"That would only make me look more suspicious. If Sullivan suspects something, my unexplained absence at the office would only put a bigger target on me."

"So call in sick. Get the flu. And get a hotel room."

"I'll be okay. I can do this. And I want to help."

Dean knew there was no use arguing with her. He'd learned that lesson early in their relationship. When April set her mind to something, she planted firm feet.

"Fine. Just lay low and be careful. Please."

"I will. I promise."

Dean knew it was a lie but didn't fight her on it.

She tossed back the rest of her bourbon. She then reached over and squeezed the top of his hand. "Thank you for coming. I mean it. I didn't know where else to turn. Even though I'm still freaked out, I feel much better having you here."

FIVE

Ben Dawson climbed the stairs to the second floor of his dumpy apartment complex. It was a few minutes after midnight. He'd just left the law school library. As a third-year law student at UT, he was pushing himself hard to finish strong. But he was ready to be done with law school and start working on real cases with real clients, and finally make real money. His escalating law school debt felt insurmountable at the moment.

He opened the door to his apartment and was greeted by the sound of the TV on in the small living room. His roommate, Mike, was sitting on the sofa, drinking a beer and eating pizza. Mike was a grad student studying economics. A good guy, although a bit sloppy. His eyes were glued to the TV.

"What's up, man?" Ben said.

"This is so crazy," Mike said, nodding toward the screen.

Ben turned to look at the television. A news channel was showing a chaotic scene with a hell of a lot of police around.

"What happened?" he asked.

Mike turned to him, frowned. "You seriously don't know?"

Ben shook his head. "I've been in the library all night."

"Dude. Someone assassinated Senator Carson tonight. Right here in Austin."

"You kidding?"

"Nah, man. It's insane!"

Ben immediately thought of his brother Eric and wondered if he was neck-deep in the thick of it all. Most likely. The FBI would be involved. He considered giving Eric a call but felt too tired. Besides, if Eric was on the job, he had no time to talk to his kid brother right now. He would send a text later to check in with him. He also thought of Dean. As a reporter, he was also probably on the scene. Ben would not be sending him a text. He was still ticked at him. He couldn't believe his brother had skipped out on their dad's funeral.

"There's pizza in the kitchen," Mike mentioned. "Help yourself."

"Thanks."

Ben shifted around the sofa and walked down the short hallway to his tiny bedroom. He was eager to live in something bigger and nicer. The three job offers he had on the table all had terrific first-year salaries. He and his fiancée, Jenna, would easily be able to get a nice apartment or maybe even rent a house. Jenna was excited about that. She had an energetic Labradoodle named Dilly and really wanted a yard. Ben set his backpack on the carpet, walked into the bathroom. He took a quick peek at himself in the mirror. His dark hair was disheveled from sleeping in the library. He put his hands under the water and then ran his fingers through his hair. His eyes drifted down to a collection of photographs that were stuck in the corners of his mirror. A couple were of him and Jenna together. At ACL last year, enjoying live music. Kayaking on Lady Bird Lake. There was a photo of him golfing with his two brothers on a trip to Scottsdale three summers ago. And then a photo of his father when his dad was his same age.

He pulled that photograph from the mirror and brought it closer to his face. His father was wearing a yellow T-shirt and jeans and holding a fishing pole. Ben's eyes went from the photo up to the mirror, where he stared at himself. He looked almost identical to his father. Same hair. Same square jaw. Same eyes. It was uncanny. Ben had been the only one to follow in his dad's footsteps. He'd always thought they would one day practice law together. Maybe even open their own firm. But that fantasy had drowned at the bottom of a lake four months ago.

After a quick shower, Ben threw on a wrinkled T-shirt and gym shorts, grabbed a slice of cold pizza from the kitchen, and then perched himself at his bedroom desk. He pulled his laptop from his backpack. He wanted to see if one of his law school classmates had sent him a paper from class. While searching for it, he noticed an email in his inbox from the law school registrar. He opened it up and found his student loan statement attached. He regularly received the statements and always hated reviewing them. Every time he did, the number got bigger. Ben squinted at the screen and leaned forward. But this time was way different.

What the hell? His student loan balance was zero. That wasn't right. Just a week ago, the balance had been over $110,000. So what had happened? It was clearly a mistake. He would call the registrar first thing in the morning to straighten it out. And then go back to being a deeply indebted law school student.

SIX

Eric Dawson stood at the head of the conference table. It was nearly two in the morning. The room was stuffed with federal agents. They sat and stood on all sides of a huge table that was covered in wrinkled fast-food wrappers and stacks of empty coffee cups. It had already been a hell of a long night. It felt like half of Austin was on lockdown, as every branch of security—FBI, CIA, Secret Service, Homeland Security, and local police—tried to cohesively work together to figure out what the hell had happened tonight. It was complete chaos. Collectively, they'd gotten nowhere in the four-and-a-half hours since a sniper bullet had killed a presidential candidate. The FBI director had kept Eric in charge. This was his city, so he would call the shots. For now. He had the entire force of the Bureau at his disposal. Eric could only hope something significant turned up before he had to face the TV cameras at a scheduled press conference in a few hours. The director was all but demanding it.

Eric crossed his arms, half listening as one of his agents ticked off details of a preliminary ballistics report. It was undoubtedly a professional sniper kill. Their computer experts were running numbers through their software right now to try to determine the exact angle, distance, height, and every other way you could look at such a thing. There were so many surrounding buildings that it could take them a week just to figure out the location of the shot, much less who might have pulled the trigger. Eric now had more than one hundred agents currently going door-to-door in the area. He rubbed his eyes. Fatigue was choking him. And he couldn't stop thinking about his man, Nelson, who'd gotten caught in the cross fire. The agent had survived emergency surgery. But it was still touch and go. Eric had personally gone to the agent's home two hours ago to deliver the news to his wife. Hillary Nelson had collapsed in his arms at hearing that her husband was fighting for his life. He could hear their newborn crying in the background. It was a punch to the gut. He hated the thought that the child might grow up fatherless.

Eric thought of his own wife, Tina. He doubted she would collapse in anyone's arms right now at hearing that her husband had taken a bullet. Their move to Austin had been the catalyst for their current spiral. Tina had given him an ultimatum a year ago. She had to be in Texas to provide better care for her mother, who was battling dementia, and she wasn't going without their boys. Eric had eventually caved. While he was empathetic to his wife's situation with her mother, he was still resentful. His career had been skyrocketing in DC. He was being promoted at rapid speed. But it had stalled in Austin over the past year. Their fighting about it had grown so consistently intense, Tina had asked for the separation. She suggested it would be easier to figure things out without living in the tension every moment of the day. Eric had reluctantly agreed.

Still, he was surprised Tina had not at least texted to check on him. That stung like hell. He still loved her. And he didn't want a divorce.

The agent giving the ballistics report sat as all eyes returned to Eric.

"That's all for now," he said. "Stick with your assignments. Do your jobs. Play well with others. I know that may be the most challenging aspect of this right now. Everything we're doing is being scrutinized. Try not to piss off too many people. Remember, everyone has a phone with a video camera. But don't let that stop you from finding the shooter. We'll meet here again at noon."

The agents all gathered their jackets, reports, and coffee cups, then filed out of the room. Eric's right-hand man, Special Agent Tim Brewster, remained behind and walked over to him. Brewster was a thick man around the same age, with short blond hair. He used to wrestle in college and was fiercely loyal to Eric.

"Just received this from Krieger a few minutes ago," he said.

Brewster handed him a digital tablet. Agent Krieger was a team leader. On the screen was a security photo of a thirtysomething bearded man wearing glasses, a black knit cap, and a brown UPS uniform.

"UPS?" Eric asked.

"Yes. This guy delivered packages tonight to the Frost Bank Tower. The security guard said it wasn't one of their regular guys. It was the first time he'd seen him. We ran the name. Nothing turned up. I mean, nothing. So we believe it was fake. And a UPS rep just told us they have no official record of his employment."

Eric felt his adrenaline kick in. "We been on the roof?"

"Krieger and his crew are up there right now. They haven't found anything yet. Krieger says it definitely has a position to make the shot."

"We have any other security footage of this guy?"

"Not yet. But we're searching other cameras from the surrounding block. I'm sure something will turn up."

"I want to personally speak to the security guard who interacted with him."

"We're bringing him over here now."

"Good. There's something else that's been bothering me."

"What's that?"

"Whoever did this only had a second to identify the target and take the shot. The window was minuscule. All four SUVs left the fundraiser through a private back entrance to the property. Only our team, Secret Service, and Carson's staff would've known who got into which vehicle. But our shooter was clearly locked in on the third Suburban. He had no time to scan all vehicles."

"You're thinking someone fed him the information?"

"Maybe. I want you to get a list of everyone who was there when Carson got into the vehicle. And then look into each of them. But do it quietly and offline."

"You got it."

The mention of the Frost Bank Tower unexpectedly made Eric think about his father. The law firm where his dad had been a partner for years had their offices in the same building. Eric exhaled, his mind lingering there a moment. There had been one semi-positive about moving back to Texas last year. While he might never forgive the man for what he'd done to him and his brothers growing up, Eric had still wanted his own sons to know their grandfather. Especially since Tina's father had passed away before they were born. His boys had enjoyed being around the man. Eric had gotten to see a side of his father he'd never experienced himself growing up.

Playful. Fun-loving. Supportive.

Too bad it was so short-lived.

SEVEN

Yusuf Demir sat at the very end of the bar of an Irish pub called the Dead Rabbit, one of dozens of drinking hot spots and music venues along Austin's Sixth Street. The bartender was currently calling for last round. It was a few minutes after two in the morning. But most of the patrons ignored him and seemed adamant about continuing to party. An instrumental Irish group had just wrapped up playing live music for several hours on a small stage. The whole bar district outside remained lively even at this hour. It seemed that a national travesty could not dampen young people's desire to still have a good time. The bar felt politically split. Some voiced their glee that Carson was dead and were even drunkenly toasting to it. Others were angry and upset. This had caused a few dustups between groups. It had all been very amusing for him to watch.

Demir had grabbed his current perch several hours ago, where he'd been sipping expensive vodka and monitoring a couple of TVs. Gone was the fake beard, black knit cap, and glasses. He now looked completely different, with his wig of long black hair running well past his shoulders, a clean-shaven chin, tinted sunglasses, blue jeans, and a denim jacket. He would be regularly changing his appearance, just to be safe. On a normal job, he would've immediately bolted out of town. But his contract required him to remain available for the next forty-eight hours. It seemed the power players who were paying his bill wanted to ensure there were no loose ends.

Demir didn't mind. He liked the risk. He loved the cat and mouse. It was thrilling to remain in a city that was now being flooded with police organizations. So far, no reports of any true leads. And they wouldn't find anything. He'd been so careful to cover his tracks. Even after they discovered his presence at the Frost Bank Tower—which he expected would happen quickly—it would still lead them nowhere. He was a ghost and had the contacts and expertise to stay that way.

So he calmly sat, watched, and waited.

Although the sound on the TVs was muted, he'd followed the subtitles on both screens. At this point, the news channels were showing the same video clips, and reporters were basically repeating themselves. But he knew things would accelerate come morning. He'd turned over his own video footage. He looked forward to it. While he'd terminated many important business leaders and foreign dignitaries over the years, Demir knew this one would carry extra weight and garner global coverage. Most had expected his target to win the US presidency and become the most powerful person in the world.

Demir turned when he heard another obnoxious political toast behind him. A college-age guy was standing up on his wobbly chair. This was met with more jeers, drunken threats, and the beginnings of another tussle.

He smiled. This was fun.

EIGHT

Bryson Carter left Costa Rica and set up shop in a remote warehouse near the Austin airport. This gave him and his team easy access in and out of the city. There was an army of them now. Six men, three women. More than they'd taken with them to Costa Rica, where two guys remained and continued to work on Jerry Dawson. It had taken them thirty-one days to track him down. Much longer than expected. He'd been good at hiding. But getting him to break and reveal his secrets had been more difficult than they'd anticipated. The man appeared to be willing to suffer horribly and possibly even die to guard the truth. They'd brought him to the brink of death several times, only to nurse him back to health each time. He was no good to them dead. And they weren't killers. Dawson's willingness to put his own life on the line led them to believe he was protecting someone he deeply loved. Love was the only emotion powerful enough to help a man endure this kind of pain and suffering. But they'd found no evidence of someone like this in his life before he'd disappeared four months ago. They were again searching.

They would keep at him using every trick in their book. The human spirit could only endure so much for so long. But unfortunately, they didn't have the luxury of time. Their powerful client had made that very clear. They needed the man to break soon, or they needed to find something on their own. Otherwise, the operation was in jeopardy.

Dawson had lived and worked in Austin nearly his entire life. There were a lot of paths for them to pursue, people to address and watch, and angles for them to monitor. It was tedious work. But they were paid extremely well to be tedious. Every associate on his former legal team was being investigated. Phone records. Bank records. Computer records. So far, none of them stood out as a connecting player. Nevertheless, each of them was being routinely observed. They would all be watched closely until they found something.

Dawson had three ex-wives. His first ex died a year ago. They'd been divorced for seventeen years. She never remarried. His second ex-wife lived in Florida. They'd been married for three years before things ended a decade ago. She was remarried to a member of the coast guard. They'd found no evidence of communication between them over the past few years. She was not a likely candidate. He'd been married to a third woman for only six months before things ended five years ago. She was twenty years younger than him and was now in Los Angeles pursuing an acting career. According to his work associates, Dawson had never even mentioned her. Some didn't even know she existed. Still, they sent someone out to California to check her out.

Dawson had three sons with his first wife. The oldest was a special agent with the FBI and ran the Austin office. He had an impeccable service record. This made him an unlikely prospect. For obvious reasons, they would need to be more careful around him. The second son was a reporter with a local online investigative publication. There had been a major uptick in communication with this son in the few months before Dawson had disappeared. But not much in the year previously. The third son was a law student at the University of Texas. Dawson seemed closest to him. They had regularly texted until the man's supposed death. But they found no evidence of communication with any of the sons since he'd disappeared.

They were again digging into every relationship in the man's life. An exercise they'd been through already during their initial search for him. But now they were going back for a second round. They'd missed something. Experience told them no one goes at something like he did completely alone. His was a complex and impressive scheme. Someone else had to have been involved. They had to find this person.

NINE

April had barely slept and was back at the office before sunrise. The floor was nearly empty. She found one first-year associate sleeping at his desk, his face buried in a mound of paperwork. He'd obviously been there all night. She didn't wake him. She still had an hour before most of the staff began arriving. The lawyers would usually stumble in closer to nine o'clock. It was common for attorneys with families to spend time with their kids in the morning, because they were all expected to stay at the office deep into the night. April couldn't remember the last time she'd left before ten unless it was for a law firm function. She was counting on the office being quiet this morning.

Although she'd promised Dean to lay low, April knew it was impossible. So did Dean. It went against her true nature. She'd always been someone who liked to take control and make things happen. That was how she'd gotten a full-ride volleyball scholarship as a setter to San Diego State and earned third-team All-American honors. It was how she'd graduated second in her law school class, something that still made her angry. She'd never believed the guy who got top billing had better grades. He had always been a cocky jerk who lacked her work ethic. But he had one thing going for him that she couldn't match: His father was one of the biggest donors to the law school.

April went straight to her office, placed her workbag behind her desk but didn't turn on any lights. She didn't want to draw attention to herself. She then traveled the long hallway to the corner of the floor, where her boss had an office even larger than her one-bedroom apartment in a high-rise four blocks away. The space contained a round conference table and had a full sitting area with two leather couches. She could see half the city from his corner-window view. April could feel her fingers begin to shake as she approached his door. Was she really going to do this? She'd considered trying to anonymously get the text message exchange between Sullivan and Rainer to the FBI. But she knew there was a good chance they would be able to trace it back to her somehow. She wasn't willing to risk that just yet. Not until she knew more about what was going on and how it might impact her future as a lawyer. So she had to do this. She was tired of randomly searching online client files for clues and connections. That felt like a needle-in-the-haystack pursuit. And she knew the best place to possibly find real evidence was right in front of her.

She paused a moment outside Sullivan's glass office door. She took a second to listen for movement in either direction down the hallway. She didn't hear anything. He was not known to arrive early unless he had to be in court for trial. He would often come in around ten, but he would stay later than most. This was why most of his team worked themselves into the ground. None of them would dare to chance leaving before him, or else they'd suffer the consequences. Sullivan could be a real hard-ass. He pushed them all to the limit and was often callous in the way he treated the associates. But was he also a killer? April couldn't wrap her mind around that.

After taking a deep breath and letting it out slowly, she put her fingers on the door handle. It was unlocked, which was no surprise. No one was stupid enough to enter his office uninvited and potentially face his wrath. But here she was. Ms. Stupid. The overhead lights were off, but there were two lamps on in both corners that cast warm light throughout the office suite. Her heart began to race as she fully entered and hurried over to his massive desk in the corner. Sullivan's desktop was always neat and tidy. His assistant, Bertha, made sure of it. She'd been with Sullivan for twenty years. Most of the associates joked that Bertha was the real head of the firm. She could be intimidating. But she'd been sweet with April from the beginning. Bertha had a daughter who played high school volleyball, so the two of them always had something to chat about.

April started with a stack of files on the corner of the desk. She quickly began opening and sorting through them. She had no idea what she was looking for and knew there was probably no chance of her finding anything within them. She got to the end of the files with nothing to show for it. She shifted fully around his desk until she was standing behind it. This made her heart beat even faster. She could smell the high-priced cognac he always drank, along with the pungent odor of his cigars. While smoking was prohibited in the building, Sullivan played by his own rules.

The rest of his desktop held his computer, a firm phone, and a few knickknacks. She reached down and pulled open his center drawer. It was loaded with the usual office supplies: pens, pencils, notepads, paper clips, rubber bands. There was a stack of business cards. She sat in his plush office chair—one she'd heard cost $20,000—and began swiftly shuffling through the business cards. She was keeping an eye out for anyone with a first or last name of Rainer. But no such luck. So she shifted to what her true mission was at the moment: Sullivan's computer. Two months ago, Sullivan had called her late at night from DC, where he was involved in a big trial for a client. He asked her to go into his office and access something from his computer. He gave her his password. Had he changed it since then? She was about to find out. She put her hand on his computer mouse and woke the computer screen. Then she nervously typed in the same password. It worked. She was inside his computer.

April searched his desktop screen for any file folders that looked like they might be connected to the Carson situation. She found nothing.

She then went to his email and began scanning. She found nothing immediate that identified anyone as Rainer. So she did a quick search. Still nothing. No Rainer. She opened his work calendar and reviewed it. Everything looked like standard firm appointments. Nothing that popped out to her as a connection point. Finally, she opened up his "Messages" folder, which was connected to his phone's text messages. She felt her adrenaline spike. That was where she found something. Within the same text message strand as the other exchange between her boss and Rainer was a new message.

Sullivan: Need to meet. 1pm tomorrow. JW Marriott bar.

Rainer: Copy that.

The message exchange was from last night at 11:37 p.m. She pulled out her phone and snapped a photo. Then she heard a voice boom out from the office door, scaring the hell out of her.

"Who's in here?"

April's eyes darted up. Bertha! She was a larger woman. Not heavy-set, but more like a former powerlifter. The woman's girth blocked the whole doorframe. April felt a wave of panic seize her. She was cursing on repeat in her head. She had to get moving. Before Bertha turned on the main overhead lights and completely exposed her. She clicked to close his Messages app. But she didn't have time to shut down his computer when the office lights suddenly blinded her.

"April?" Bertha asked, frowning, head tilted.

April swallowed, stood. "Hi, Bertha. Good morning."

She wondered if the woman could hear the shakiness in her voice. Or see that her hands were trembling at her sides.

"What are you doing in here?" Bertha asked, brow furrowed.

"Searching for the Canton file," she replied, thinking quickly. "Edward took it from me last night."

April moved around to the front of the desk and again began to search through the stack of files on the corner.

"Canton?" Bertha asked. "But you're not on Canton anymore."

Bertha was sharp. She knew every move Sullivan made. So she, of course, knew her boss had removed her from the Canton case.

"Right. But I think I left some of my notes for another client in there."

"Which client?" Bertha asked, eyes narrow.

"Connor Fields," April said without hesitation. The only way she would get out of this unscathed was to exude calm and confidence.

"Edward took the Canton file home with him last night."

"Oh, okay. No big deal. I'll get it from him later."

April began moving toward the door. She took quick, shallow breaths, and begged her face to somehow smile and act nonchalant. She had no idea if it was working because Bertha was still staring her down. The woman guarded Sullivan's office like a bouncer at a popular nightclub. No one entered without her approval. So she was clearly not pleased to find April circumventing that restriction. For a moment, April wondered if Bertha knew the truth about what had happened with Senator Carson. Could she know her boss might somehow be wrapped up in the assassination?

April was also concerned Bertha was making no move to allow her to freely walk out of the office as she approached. Was the older woman going to try to pin her down until security arrived? Were they about to have a physical confrontation? April had to think fast, and she knew exactly which direction she needed to go.

"Hey, I saw Westlake High took down Dripping Springs in straight sets the other night. How many kills did Natasha have?"

Natasha was Bertha's daughter. Westlake was where she went to high school. For fun, April had been keeping up with their volleyball matches online. Natasha was a star player and was likely headed to a major school on scholarship. April said a quick, desperate prayer this might be her get-out-of-jail-free card. It seemed to work. The hard lines in Bertha's face began immediately smoothing out.

"She crushed her school record," Bertha said, grinning. "And she did it in only three sets. They just kept feeding her the ball. It was a joy to watch."

"Wonderful," April replied. "She sure is special. If I'd had half her talent, I might still be out there playing on one of the women's circuits. Is she close to choosing a college?"

"She's down to three schools. UCLA, Florida, and Nebraska. I want her to stay local, of course, but my girl has a mind of her own. She just wants to spread her wings and fly."

"Can't blame her for that. I wanted the same thing."

Bertha was all smiles now. She cleared the door and let April exit. They spoke a few more minutes about her daughter and volleyball before April finally managed to step away and head back to her office. Shutting the door behind her, she finally took a deep breath. She felt like she'd been holding it for the last ten minutes. She was afraid Bertha was going to notice the sweat dripping down her pits the entire time they were talking. That was way too close a call. While she did find something valuable on Sullivan's computer, April now had to live with the additional fear that Bertha would mention something to her boss. But her mind immediately returned to the text message exchange between Sullivan and Rainer. They were meeting today. If she played her cards right, she should have some answers about this person's identity soon. That felt like a big step toward getting to the truth.

TEN

Dean met with his editor early the next morning at Kerbey Lane Cafe. He'd been up most of the night. Part of that was because he was searching everywhere online for a connection between Edward Sullivan and the mystery person named Rainer. But most of his tossing and turning was the result of him trying to process the mention of the name "Dawson" at the beginning of the text message change. *Dawson still hasn't broken. I've known him twenty years.* Dean couldn't wrap his mind around any scenario where they were discussing his father. The man was dead. There was a funeral. End of story. But then who else could Sullivan have been talking about?

Harvey sat across the booth from him. He was still in his running gear: a black jogging outfit with a black headband. His boss hit the downtown running trail by six each morning. Harvey required little sleep. He said if he got five hours, he was good to go. Even though he was thirty-five years Dean's senior, his boss made him feel like the older man. Dean had regretfully accepted an invite to run with him once, but he couldn't keep up the pace. It was embarrassing. The silver-haired man was a machine, both on the trail and in the newsroom.

Kerbey Lane was still pretty empty at seven in the morning. They sat in a quiet booth in the corner. A redheaded waitress delivered two hot cups of coffee.

"This couldn't wait until the office?" Harvey asked, taking a sip.

"No, sir. I may have something big. Bigger than big."

"Well, don't make me beg, son. Let's have it."

Dean told him about his late-night meetup with April and then showed him the text message exchange between Sullivan and Rainer.

Harvey was quiet for a long moment. "This is potentially big," he finally said, putting his coffee down. "How's April handling it?"

"She's scared. I told her to lay low, but I doubt she'll do that. She's never been one to sit back. I just hope she's careful."

"You okay seeing her? It's been a while, right?"

"A year. It was . . . good. Confusing, but good."

Dean had confided in Harvey about his relationship with April and the difficulty of how badly he'd allowed it to end. His mother's passing and the breakup had caused havoc in every area of his life. Dean had produced little in the news-story category for nearly two months after his mom's death. And the one story he finally did produce had nearly ended his career. It was only Harvey's grace that allowed him to still have a job. Most other news organizations would've terminated him immediately. Harvey was more than just a boss to him. Dean was eager to reward the man's loyalty with a bigger story.

"Do you know anyone over at Michaels & Peterson?" Dean asked.

"Yes, I've met a couple of partners here and there at various events. Big money firm. Important clients. Of course, I'd also met your dad. I don't personally know Edward Sullivan. But I certainly know his reputation as a powerful player." Harvey stared down at Dean's phone again. "This exchange is stunning to read. If any of this is truly connected with what happened last night, we need to handle this with extreme care. We should consider going to the police or the FBI."

"I urged April to do that. But she refuses to make that move yet."

"Okay. But let's keep a very tight circle. Understood?"

"Yes, sir. I agree."

"You find any leads on this Rainer?"

"Not yet. I've been searching, but so far, I've come up with nothing."

"I'll go on my own hunt when I get back to the office."

"Okay, thanks."

"Dawson still hasn't broken," Harvey said, reciting the first line of the text. He looked up at Dean with arched eyebrows.

"They can't be talking about him, Harvey. It makes zero sense."

"How long had your father been partners with Sullivan?"

"More than twenty years," Dean admitted.

"That's a hell of a coincidence." Harvey leaned back in the booth, crossed his arms. "You told me the police never recovered his body, right?"

"Yes, but what are you suggesting? He faked his own death?"

"Or someone could've staged it."

"But . . . why?"

"Hell if I know. I'm just spitballing here."

"Believe me, I've been wrestling with this all night. But I just can't fathom my father faking his death. We'd just started rebuilding the relationship. I know he was trying to do the same with Eric and Ben. I was giving him a real chance, even though everything inside me told me to not open that door. That I would regret it. But I did it anyway. So for him to do something like this would be cruel, even for him."

"I understand. He could've been forced to do it. And this could all be speculative nonsense. But we need to chase down the remote possibility. At this point, it's still a potential component of the story. And it could be the biggest part."

ELEVEN

Eric pulled up to the curb in front of his house a few minutes before eight that morning. Since he and Tina had separated a couple weeks ago, he'd been staying at a crummy weekly-rate motel nearby. But he'd remained committed to taking his boys to school every morning. As much as possible, he wanted things to feel normal for them. Their house was a small gray-brick model that looked nearly identical to all the others on the block. His government paycheck couldn't afford them much, and Tina had stopped working altogether when they'd moved back to Texas. She said she needed to be available to her mother full-time. His mother-in-law was getting more confused and sometimes even getting lost. Because of this, Tina had recently taken away her car. His wife had wanted to move her mother into the house with them, but Eric had put his foot down. He said there was no way that would help their marriage. This had only caused more tension between them. He wasn't sure how they would resolve it all.

He killed the engine and sat in his Bronco for a moment. He was so tired. He'd remained at the office the entire night and never made it back to his motel room. Unfortunately, there had been no new developments overnight. They could find no trace of evidence left behind by the sniper at the Frost Bank Tower. And finding other area security footage of the man had been difficult. He was clearly a professional.

Which made them believe this was not a crazy lone-gunman operation. The sniper had been put in play by others. Their list of suspects who could potentially be behind the assassination was growing by the hour. It was currently at twenty. Seven international terrorist organizations. Four white supremacy groups. Three other violent domestic outfits. And then the usual long list of enemy countries. That felt daunting.

Eric got out of his Bronco and walked up the front sidewalk to the house. He knocked on the door and waited. He could hear his two rambunctious boys running around inside. Grayson was ten, Will was eight. He heard one of his boys yell, "Freeze! Put your hands up!" This made him smile. The boys constantly destroyed the house with their boisterous play habits. Their favorite game was FBI—much to his wife's chagrin—where one of them got to be a special agent, while the other was a bad guy who had to hide. Tina never liked the idea of one of her sons pretending to hunt down the other with a play gun and shooting him dead. She felt it desensitized them to violence. Eric had to remind her she'd married a damn FBI agent.

Will answered the door. "Daddy!"

Eric scooped him up. "Hey, buddy. You and your brother ready?"

"Almost. Let me get my backpack."

Eric put Will down and watched him race back inside. Eric could smell the coffee brewing. He missed the aroma. He missed the ease of having a kitchen. He missed his comfortable bed. Tina made her way over to the front door still wearing her flannel pajamas. Her blond hair was a bit disheveled, and she wore little makeup. But she was still a stunner. Always had been. He also missed her.

"You look like hell," she said.

"Been a long night."

"Don't forget to pick them up from football practice tonight."

And that was all he got from her. He was running point on the biggest investigation in the world right now, and his wife couldn't manage to offer him the slightest bit of empathy. She really had grown to hate his job. It hadn't always been that way. When they were first dating, she found his work exciting. She said she liked the idea of him keeping the world safer. But things dramatically changed when they had kids.

Tina stepped out of the way as both of his boys came running out with their backpacks. He said goodbye and loaded them up. After making a quick stop by McDonald's on the way to school, something forbidden by their mother, he hugged them both at drop-off and watched them race into the building. He was barely back inside his Bronco when Agent Brewster rang him on his cell phone.

"Yeah?" he answered.

"How close are you to the office, boss?"

"Ten minutes. Why?"

"A new development. Get here as fast as you can."

Eric punched hard on the gas.

Eric returned to the office just in time to find most of his team huddled in a conference room around a wall of TV monitors. The news anchors were all talking about the same thing. Major news had broken out of Mexico. A CBS reporter said the Zeta Cartel, one of the biggest and deadliest drug organizations in the world, was now taking responsibility for the assassination of Senator Carson, and they claimed to have evidence they wanted to share with the world. The cartel had just minutes ago released a video on YouTube. The news anchor warned viewers the video was graphic. Although they could not yet verify its authenticity, the reporter said they felt an obligation to share it with their audience as newsworthy coverage. Apparently every news channel felt the same obligation because the video was simultaneously popping up on every screen.

Eric was suddenly looking through what appeared to be the high-powered scope of a sniper rifle. He felt his chest tighten. The footage rolled, and he began to recognize the scene. The string of black Suburbans in front of the Four Seasons hotel. The protective detail rushing around it, including his own team. Eric cursed. It was incredible footage. His heart began to race when he saw a clear shot of Agent Nelson in a group circling the third Suburban. Carson then appeared from the vehicle, paused, turned, the screen jolted a touch, and a moment later, Eric watched as the senator's head exploded in violent fashion. Then the screen went black.

There was collective cursing in the conference room.

Brewster stepped over to him. "What do you think?"

"Looks authentic. But they weren't even on our list."

"They probably should have been. Carson has been making campaign promises about cracking down hard on the cartels."

"Yeah, but both sides have been saying the same thing. And we know this was likely the work of a professional. Hiring a professional is not usually the MO for the cartels. They like to chop heads and limbs off."

"True. But how else would they have gotten the video?"

"That's what we need to find out ASAP."

TWELVE

Dean met midmorning with the detective who'd investigated his father's death in the dirt parking lot of Rosie's Tamale House, a hole-in-the-wall Mexican restaurant on the outskirts of Austin near Lake Travis, where his dad kept his boat. Goodson, a hefty fiftysomething man with a serious buzz cut to go along with a serious brow, had been with the Travis County Sheriff's Office for over two decades. Goodson had reluctantly agreed over the phone to give Dean no more than five minutes of his busy time. And he seemed agitated with even that arrangement.

"Thanks for meeting with me," Dean said.

"What's this about again?"

"I'm doing a story about deaths on the lake."

Dean didn't want to muddy the conversation by telling the detective this was about his father. So he never mentioned his own last name. He figured Goodson might speak more freely without that tidbit.

"What's so interesting about that?"

"Lots of people here in Austin love the lake."

Goodson spit on the ground. "Yeah, and they give me headaches."

"There were twelve deaths on Lake Travis this past year?"

"Something like that."

"Is there a common theme?"

"What do you think? Folks can't seem to get on a boat without getting drunk off their asses. Inebriated people do the dumbest things."

"Right. Like the case you were on four months ago. Jerry Dawson?"

Goodson nodded. "Yeah. Lawyer. Really nice boat. Expensive."

Dean had never been on his father's boat despite receiving several invites. He knew Eric had taken his boys out before. And Ben had gone out with Jenna.

"He was by himself?"

"Yep. Late-night cruise on the water. A real winner of a guy. We found four empty bottles of high-priced bourbon and half a dozen empty beer cans. I guess it's stressful trying to figure out how to spend all that lawyer money. You gotta drink the blues away on your hundred-thousand-dollar ski boat."

His father had always been a functioning alcoholic. But Dean had been surprised to find out what happened on the boat. His father had sworn he'd given up drinking. He'd claimed he wanted to be a better man. A better dad. A better grandfather. Obviously, these were all lies. The story of his life.

"So he drowned, right?" Dean asked.

"Yep. We believe he slipped, banged his head on the side of the boat, fell overboard, and was so drunk and dazed, maybe unconscious, he had no chance."

"You found blood?"

"Blood and tissue that tests confirmed belonged to him."

"But you couldn't find his body?"

"Not yet. It's out there somewhere."

"Is that normal?"

Goodson shrugged. "The lake is sixty-four miles long. Boat could've been drifting all night before someone discovered it."

"But they normally wash up eventually, right?"

"Normally. However, we did find a person who'd been missing for twelve years recently, when the lake dried out in a cove. Body had been tangled up at the bottom. We're still waiting for the lawyer to pop up on someone's boat dock somewhere. Give some kids a nice little scare. Uncle Jerry is home."

He seemed amused at himself, laughing, his belly shaking.

"Any signs of foul play involved?"

"Nope, the boat was clean, other than what I've already told you. And marina security footage showed he'd boarded alone." Goodson stared at Dean. "You sure are asking a lot of questions about this specific case."

"It's a more interesting story when there is no body."

"Well, you ain't the first person who's come by recently to ask me questions about this same dead guy. He's popular, I guess."

Dean tilted his head. "Who else?"

"Some insurance adjuster. Asked all these same annoying questions about him a few weeks ago. Wanted to know if someone else could've been on the boat with him. Or with him at the dock. All the nitty-gritty details."

Dean found it unusual that an insurance adjuster would come talk to the detective more than three months after the incident. That usually happened immediately. Could it have been someone else pretending to be an insurance adjuster? He made a mental note to call his father's insurance company when he was done with the detective.

"Detective, do you think there's any chance Jerry Dawson didn't die out there in the water?"

Goodson glared at him. "Now why the hell would you ask me that?"

"A common fantasy among rich lawyers is to fake their own deaths, flee their stressful legal responsibilities, and run off with their money."

"Hell, I don't know, kid. He would've had to have been willing to bang his own head pretty damn hard against the boat. We're not talking about a couple drops of blood. But I guess anything is possible. It's not really my job to figure that out. And I don't have the time or energy to speculate when there is no real reason for it."

THIRTEEN

April tried her best to do some actual legal work in her office the rest of the morning. She thought if she could somehow stay busy, she might be able to briefly take her mind off the stress of the situation. But it didn't work. She just stared blankly at her laptop screen while her mind churned. She made sure to steer clear of Sullivan's corner of the floor. Just the thought of interacting with the man right now caused her stomach to twist. She had no idea if Bertha had mentioned anything to her boss about her being inside his office this morning. So far, Sullivan had not stomped down the hallway to demand answers. Maybe she was in the clear. Maybe her charm with Bertha had paid off.

This had been her repeat prayer all morning.

She checked her watch. Sullivan's calendared meeting with Rainer at the JW Marriott was scheduled in one hour. She'd initially thought of trailing her boss herself but decided that was too risky after what happened with Bertha this morning. So she'd texted the info to Dean. He'd responded with some displeasure at her inability to stay away from the matter but didn't give her too hard a time. Dean knew she would never be able to do that. Her mind sat with the thought of Dean for a moment. She had to admit it was nice to be communicating with him again. It felt comfortable. Like old times. Like they'd never stopped. Dean had always had a calming way about him. She could get worked up about things—big and small—but he could bring her back to center. His tone. His words. His touch. She'd missed it. She'd missed . . . him.

April cursed, shook off this thought.

Her situation was complicated enough without bringing emotions into it.

When her stomach began to growl, April decided to head out to grab a quick sandwich nearby. Stepping out of her office, she glanced down toward the corner. She froze, cursed. Sullivan was standing right outside his own office, speaking with another partner, and looked over in her direction. They locked eyes for an awkward moment. April wasn't sure what to do. Wave? That would be stupid. His eyes were slits, his brow wrinkled. Did he know she knew what was going on? His face said he knew and was furious with her. Then again, he always looked that way. She ignored his glare, quickly turned, and headed off in the opposite direction.

She took an elevator down to the lobby and was out on a busy sidewalk a few minutes later. Most of the downtown workforce was also headed out for lunch. April would regularly frequent a sandwich shop two blocks away. They made the best Italian subs. She hadn't eaten a thing since last night—her stomach had been so tied up in knots—but she was starting to get lightheaded. Her blood sugar had dropped. She needed fuel. She paused at a streetlight with a group of others, waiting for the walk sign. She glanced to her left. A man in a black windbreaker was staring right at her from ten feet over. He was probably fortysomething, with short, curly hair. When their eyes met, he didn't look away. He just kept staring. On some level, she was used to it. She was attractive enough to get consistently hit on. But this one made her uneasy for some reason.

The walk sign flashed, and her group crossed over like a herd of cattle. A moment later, she stepped inside her favorite sandwich shop and got in line. When she got to the front, she placed her order and paid. After collecting her sandwich, she glanced back at the growing line behind her. The place was popular. Then she spotted the same curly-headed guy in the black windbreaker standing five people back. When she caught him staring again, he looked away.

April left the sandwich shop and headed back toward her office. She paused at the stoplight directly across from her building. Something made her turn around to look back over her shoulder. And there he was again. Same guy wearing the black windbreaker. Her eyes narrowed in on him. He didn't have a sandwich in his hands. Instead, both were stuffed in his jacket pockets. Why? April felt a sudden chill rush up her back. For the first time, she began to wonder if this man wasn't just a random sidewalk admirer.

Was she being followed?

FOURTEEN

Ben took a white hand towel and cleaned the bar top at Crown & Anchor Pub, where he'd been bartending the past two years. It was a quiet lunch crowd today. A few guys were playing pool in the back. Three couples sitting at tables. A small group of folks out on the patio with their dogs. Business at the pub usually picked up around two in the afternoon when their designated happy hour began every day. The college kids would start piling in. Not that he made much in tips from other students. It was the affluent families from Hyde Park that allowed him to make ends meet. Ben enjoyed the busy and loud environment of the pub. It balanced out all the isolated, silent time he spent in the library and usually helped relax him.

But Ben was anything but relaxed today. His mind was still reeling from the call he'd had with the law school registrar's office this morning. He was told the full balance paid on his student loans was not a mistake. Someone had made the payment. One of the gals in the office said a man called about a week ago, claimed he was Ben's uncle, and asked for the payment information. They did not have a name. The money was wired from a bank in the Cayman Islands. That was all they knew.

It was real. He couldn't believe it. But he also couldn't understand it. He didn't have an uncle. His mother was an only child. And while his father did once have a brother, the man had died when Ben was still in middle school. There was no one else. So who had placed the call last week and paid more than a hundred grand on his account?

Better yet, why the hell would they do it?

He kept racking his brain all morning but came up with no good answer.

Ben glanced over when a lady probably in her late forties came into the restaurant and found a stool at the end of the bar. She wore a nice white silk blouse with a black skirt. Her blond hair was perfect. She was very attractive. He set down a glass he was cleaning and wandered over to her. He noticed two things. First, the huge diamond wedding ring. It was probably four times the size of the minuscule diamond he'd just given to Jenna. Second, the woman's eyes were completely bloodshot. She'd either already been heavily drinking today, or she'd been crying hard.

"What can I get you?" Ben said, offering a smile.

She didn't return the smile. "You're Ben, right?"

He cocked his head. "Right. Do I know you?"

"No. But I know your father."

"Oh, okay." He wondered why the woman said it in the present tense. Did she not know his father had passed away? "How did you know my father?"

"We, uh . . . were friends."

She corrected herself. She sniffled and then took a tissue out of her purse to wipe her nose. His guess was she'd been crying this morning.

"Are you okay?" he asked.

She shook her head. "No, I'm a wreck."

"I'm sorry to hear that. Maybe a drink will help?"

She looked around, leaned forward on the bar, and whispered, "When was the last time you spoke to your father?"

"The day he died," he said. Who was this woman?

Her face sagged. She seemed disappointed with his answer. "You haven't spoken with him in the past couple of days?"

Was this lady crazy? What the hell?

"I'm confused. You mean, like going to his grave site and having a chat?"

Her eyes immediately watered up, and she put her face in her hands. "I'm so sorry. I shouldn't have come here. It was a mistake. I just . . . I feel desperate."

"I don't understand."

She wiped her eyes with the tissue again. "I know. He wanted to protect you, Ben. Protect you and your brothers."

"Protect us from what? What are you talking about?"

"I should go," she said, slipping off the stool. Before leaving, she pulled a piece of paper out of her purse and scribbled something on it with a pen. "I know this sounds crazy, Ben. But if you hear anything about your father in the next few days, will you please call me at this number? Day or night."

She slid it across the bar. He picked it up. A phone number. No name.

"Yeah, sure. I suppose. Who are you?"

She didn't respond. Instead, she rushed out, leaving Ben standing there, mouth wide open. What the hell was that all about?

FIFTEEN

Dean sat on a leather couch in the pristine lobby of the JW Marriott, two blocks from where the assassination had taken place last night, pretending to read a newspaper while his eyes steadily bounced around behind it. The lobby and adjoining bar area were packed with people. Dozens were sitting at tables, reclining on couches, and perched up on stools. The hotel was a popular place for business events and conferences. There were two popular restaurants on opposite ends of the main lobby. And several massive ballrooms were located on the second floor. The crowd made it easier for him to blend into the environment. He'd received a text message from April five minutes ago informing him Edward Sullivan had left the office and was on his way.

While waiting, Dean replayed everything the detective had told him about his father's drowning death. They'd found blood and tissue belonging to his father. The detective said it was not a couple of drops of blood. If his father had faked his own death, would he have badly hurt himself to do it? Or could it have been something else? Even though the detective found no evidence of anyone else on the boat, could he have been wrong? Could there have been another person with his father who tried to kill him? Was that why they'd found the blood and tissue? Meeting with the detective had only brought up more questions. A call to his father's insurance company had not helped clear up matters, either. A rep claimed they had not sent out an adjuster to speak with the authorities a few weeks ago. So who was it? And why were they asking the same questions?

Dean sighed, continued to study the faces of those men and women who were sitting by themselves in the lobby, wondering if any of them could be the mysterious Rainer. He had no idea if this person was a man or a woman yet. He checked his watch. Right at one, Sullivan entered the lobby. He was a strikingly good-looking sixty-year-old man with a full head of gray-brown hair wearing a sharp blue suit with a tie. He walked with purpose, eyes up, good posture, like someone powerful and in charge. Dean had only met the man once at a law firm banquet he'd attended with April. The partner had a charismatic personality and had rattled off several nice things he knew about him.

Because of their familiarity with each other, Dean kept the newspaper up near his eyes. He didn't need Sullivan spotting him and blowing this opportunity. Sullivan quickly passed by, walked through the rest of the lobby, and sat at the bar directly beside a fortysomething man with thinning brown hair, glasses, and wearing a black business suit. Rainer? The two men didn't shake hands, didn't slap each other on the backs, or even much acknowledge each other. They just sat there and stared straight ahead, like they didn't even know each other. But they began talking.

Hopping up from his couch spot, Dean circled the lobby and found a wall beside a fireplace to get a better view of them. He pulled out his phone, aimed, zoomed in, and began snapping photos. He then texted them to April.

Recognize him?

She immediately responded. No. Can you get close enough to hear what they're talking about?

Not without risking getting caught.

There were zero smiles from either man. Just stern faces, pinched eyebrows. A serious conversation. One that did not last long. They were done talking after fifteen minutes. Sullivan got up first and left. Dean slid back behind the protection of the fireplace. Then he peeked his head around again. Rainer took a few more minutes to finish his drink and got up from his stool. He turned to walk in Dean's direction. This was Dean's first opportunity to get a full-on view of the man's face. He looked like a college professor. Pale. Nerdy. Academic. There was something familiar about his face.

Where had he seen this man before?

Dean followed. Rainer did not leave the hotel. Instead, he walked all the way through the lobby, passed by the Italian restaurant in the corner, and headed toward the elevators. Was he staying in the hotel? Did that make him an out-of-towner? Rainer moved fully into the elevator corridor. Dean cursed. He would not be able to tell on which floor Rainer was staying without being inside the elevator with him. But he couldn't chance doing that by himself. Some good fortune arrived seconds later in the form of four guys in business suits wearing lanyards for a conference going on in the hotel, who were making a beeline toward the same elevator corridor. Dean moved in behind them.

The entire group arrived just as Rainer's elevator door sprang open. Dean remained close to the businessmen and made sure to find a position in the corner of the elevator carriage. Rainer pushed the floor button for twelve. Other buttons were pushed. Dean requested seventeen. The elevator door closed and up they went. The group of businessmen was chatting away about whatever meeting they'd just attended. Rainer had his eyes mostly locked in on his phone screen. He glanced back just once, and Dean made sure to tuck himself away. Thankfully, only one of the conference guys got off on a floor below Rainer. When the elevator arrived on twelve, Rainer stepped out. Dean waited until the very last moment before quickly pushing through the others. He stuck his hand out to block the elevator door from shutting and caused it to open again.

"This isn't seventeen," one of the guys said to him.

"Yeah, my bad. Forgot my floor."

Dean stepped out. He rapidly moved up to the hallway and cautiously stuck his head around a corner. He spotted Rainer down the long hallway. When the man made a turn at another hallway corner, Dean rushed ahead, trying to move as quietly as possible. He needed to get there before Rainer entered a room, or else he'd lose track of him. He pressed up against the next corner, again peeked around. He found Rainer standing in front of a room door. Four doors down from him was a housekeeping cart. The professor pulled out a card key, stuck it in the electronic lock, and disappeared inside.

Dean stepped in close enough to get the room number and hastily returned to his hiding place around the hallway corner. What now? He pulled out his cell phone, called the front desk, and asked them to ring room 1217. He thought he might be able to draw out Rainer's full name by faking a DoorDash order and pretending to be delivering food. When he was patched through, the phone rang four times before going to an automated hotel voicemail system. Rainer wasn't interested in answering his hotel-room phone.

All Dean could do now was wait.

SIXTEEN

Dean didn't have to wait long. Rainer was on the move again within minutes. This time, he reappeared from his hotel room with a workbag over his shoulder and pushing a silver carry-on suitcase. It looked like the man was checking out of the hotel. Dean hurried back to the elevator corridor and ducked inside the ice-and-soda-machine cove next to it. He'd already scouted out the location for this possibility. He stood in front of the soda machine, back facing the hallway, acting like he was still deciding on his selection, and listened. Rainer approached with his suitcase and then passed by him. Seconds later, Dean heard an elevator door open and shut around the corner. The professor was gone. Which was fine. Dean knew it would be impossible to follow him down twelve flights from here. But he'd thought of something else while waiting. Dean rushed back to Rainer's hotel room and located the same cleaning cart he'd spotted earlier. The maid was now stripping a bed inside a room three doors down.

"Excuse me," Dean said from the door.

She looked up. "Yes."

"Hi, this is so embarrassing. But I accidentally locked myself out of my hotel room. Is there any way you can let me inside to get my key? The name is Rainer. Room 1217."

She picked up an iPad. Dean presumed it was hotel issued and contained room information. Seeming satisfied, she looked up at him.

"Yes, of course, Mr. Rainer."

Dean now knew Rainer was a last name. Until this point, he'd been unsure.

"Thank you so much."

He followed her down the hallway, watched her place her master card key in the digital lock for 1217, and the door clicked open.

"Thank you again."

"You're welcome."

He waited until she walked off to step inside the room. And then he shut the door behind him. It was a standard hotel room with a king-size bed, a comfy chair in one corner, a dresser, and a desk. To his immediate left was a spacious bathroom. Dean began his search. He found used towels on the bathroom floor. There were a couple of empty mini-bottles of hotel shampoo and conditioner on the counter. He was looking for anything that might fully identify Rainer. An empty prescription bottle. Receipts. Subscription magazines. Had the man left something behind?

Dean knelt and searched the bathroom trash. Tissues, a used toothbrush, and a couple Snickers candy wrappers. Nothing else. He moved into the main area of the room. The bed was unmade. He searched the nightstands on both sides but found nothing worthwhile. The desk held copies of the latest *USA Today* and *The New York Times*. Hotel issued. Nothing with his name on it. The trash can in the main space was filled with empty minibar bottles. Vodka. Tequila. Whiskey. Probably ten total bottles. The professor was either an alcoholic or trying hard to manage an extraordinary level of stress. He still found nothing to identify the guy. Dean spotted a pair of brown dress shoes pressed up against the wall next to the desk. Rainer must have accidentally left them behind. He picked up the shoes, scanned them, but found nothing to identify their owner.

Moving over to the small closet, Dean slid back the mirrored door. A hotel robe on a hanger and a luggage holder folded up in a corner. No other clothes hanging in the closet. Then he noticed something on the carpet. A wadded-up clear plastic bag that dry cleaners use when returning clothes. He bent down and found that a receipt was attached.

Dean grinned. There it was. The man's full name.

Andrew Rainer.

1426 C St. SE

Washington, DC.

Andrew Rainer lived in DC. Dean pulled out his phone, eager to search for the guy.

But a sudden sound at the door stopped him. Sounded like someone was sticking a card key in the digital lock outside in the hallway. Was it the maid returning? Or hotel security? Could the maid have informed hotel staff about him? Dean thought about the brown dress shoes. Had Rainer returned to his hotel room to retrieve them? That possibility might be worse than hotel security. Dean slipped fully into the closet, and with his right hand, he began to slide the door closed. When he heard the room door fully open, he stopped tugging altogether and pulled his hand back into the darkness. A six-inch gap remained in the closet door, but he could no longer do anything about it.

He listened, hoping to hear the voice of the maid or hotel staff. He knew he could talk his way out of that. But no voices. Only footsteps on the plush carpet. Then he saw Andrew Rainer move past the closet door. Dean slipped back even farther. The man still had his workbag and rolling luggage with him. He set the luggage on the bed and unzipped it. The professor walked over to the desk, bent down to retrieve his shoes, and stuffed them inside the bag. After zipping it up, he returned the luggage to the carpet and began wheeling it back toward the door. But the man stopped right in front of the mirrored closet. Dean held his breath. Had Rainer seen him? Was that why he'd stopped? Was the guy about to slide the door open?

Dean quickly ran through possible scenarios on how to respond. The professor was a skinny, weak-looking guy. He could easily shove him down and take off running down the hallway. But was that the best option? Should he confront the guy right now with his knowledge of the potentially lethal text exchange? No. Dean knew he couldn't do that yet without exposing April. He'd promised to protect her. So he balled his fist and planned to move forward with option A. But the closet door never moved. Instead, he heard the hotel-room door open and shut. All was silent in the room again. Dean exhaled, waited a minute to make sure Rainer hadn't left anything else behind. Feeling secure, he pulled the closet door open and stepped out. That was too damn close. He got his phone out and typed the name *Andrew Rainer* into a Google search. His screen immediately filled with options. An actor whose face was not a match. A musician who was also not the same guy. But he scored big with the third person listed on the search page.

Dean cursed, realizing why he recognized the guy. He was not a professor. But who he was sent a chill through him.

Andrew Rainer. Chief of staff.

Senator Ted Lambert. Florida.

SEVENTEEN

The FBI jet had landed in Mexico City in the early afternoon. After climbing into an unmarked black SUV, Eric was immediately whisked outside the city to a rusted old warehouse in the middle of an industrial complex. From behind a one-way mirror, he watched an intense interrogation scene. A bloodied Mexican man in his early thirties sat low in a wooden chair behind a wobbly table. A bright light hung loosely from the ceiling and blinded him. Two Mexican federal agents were circling him like vultures, slapping him hard in the back of the head, and firing off questions in their foreign tongue. Eric could only understand bits and pieces. He didn't know much Spanish. But he was standing next to a CIA agent named Carlos Mendez, who was interpreting.

The tattooed man in the chair was Geraldo Cruz, a top lieutenant in the Zeta Cartel, who had claimed responsibility for the Carson assassination earlier that morning. Working together with the Federal Ministerial Police (PFM)—Mexico's FBI—the CIA had pulled Cruz off the streets a few hours ago. Mendez had explained to Eric that they'd been following him for several weeks. Cruz apparently had a mistress he regularly met with in Mexico City. A dangerous mistress, because she happened to be the young girlfriend of Alfredo Rincon, the head of the Zetas. She often traveled to Mexico City for lavish shopping trips.

If the secret sexual excursions were discovered, Cruz would likely have his skin peeled off. Probably the girlfriend's, too. Mendez said the CIA had been waiting to pick him up and leverage their knowledge of his affair. When news broke this morning about the Zetas, the CIA knew it was the right moment.

Eric stared through the dirty glass at Cruz. The man's lips were swollen. One eye was severely gashed. And he was sweating profusely. Eric was also sweating. It was hot as hell inside this warehouse. It was like the temperature had jumped twenty degrees the moment they flew across the US border. A Mexican agent in the dark room apparently didn't like one of Cruz's responses, as he grabbed his captive by his long, greasy hair and slammed his nose into the table. Blood spattered and hit the see-through glass, inches from Eric, causing him to turn away.

"They do things differently this side of the border," Mendez mentioned.

"Do you think he'll talk?"

"He'll talk. Just have to be patient."

Eric checked his watch. He didn't have much time for patience. Fortunately, after another twenty minutes of brutal beatings, the man began spilling his guts. Cruz claimed the Zetas had nothing to do with the assassination of Senator Carson. He said one of their attorneys apparently called his boss early this morning and told him there was a $10 million offer on the table. All they had to do was take responsibility and share the video. Cruz had no idea who was making the offer. The attorney said the deal was sent through secretive back channels. His boss took the deal. The Zetas would gladly own responsibility for the assassination. Rincon felt it would strike a necessary measure of fear in any other politicians who were threatening to take them on.

"Do you believe him?" Eric asked Mendez.

Mendez nodded. "We've had assets in the right places with the Zetas the past few weeks. We would've heard if there was any activity connected to what happened in Austin last night. But there was nothing from our sources. Which is why the news caught us off guard this morning."

"Can we get to their attorney?"

"We can try. But they have dozens of attorneys. It will take time."

Eric stared at the beaten man, tried to process this new information. If true, someone with extraordinary financial means just attempted to throw them off the trail. To give the FBI a nice, tidy package that might satisfy international interest and shorten their investigative efforts. The drug cartels already had targets on them. Adding the prominent assassination of a US politician to the list would change nothing.

It was a smart and calculated effort. If it had worked.

Eric's phone buzzed. Agent Brewster back in Austin.

"Yeah?" Eric answered.

"How's it going there?"

"I've picked up a few new interrogation techniques."

"I bet."

"What do you got?"

"Just sent you something. Take a look."

Eric opened a message on his phone. On the screen were security pictures of a man standing at an airport counter. Eric scrolled through them with a finger. He was an ordinary-looking individual. Short black hair. Goatee. Eyes behind stylish spectacles. Black leather coat. Black bag over his shoulder.

"What is this?" Eric asked.

"These were taken at Toronto Pearson two days ago. This man boarded an Air Canada Flight 409 to El Paso. First class. One-way ticket."

"Who is he?"

"He flew under the name Liam Martin, a Canadian citizen. However, when he landed in El Paso, he rented a vehicle under a different identity. Martin Bouchard. US citizen. I just sent you those pics, too. He dropped the rental car off in Austin the same evening. Twenty-four hours before the assassination."

"You run these images through Interpol?"

"Yes, and we believe we've got a match."

"Tell me."

"Yusuf Demir. Also known as the Caracal."

Eric cursed. "Are you kidding me?"

"It's a seventy-two percent match. Which leaves some room for uncertainty until you overlap it with his travel logistics. I think we've got our guy, boss."

Eric had heard of the Turkish assassin. You don't spend ten years in DC without becoming familiar with the most famous killers around the globe. If Yusuf Demir was truly the man who fired the bullet that killed Carson last night, it had just greatly narrowed the field of who could possibly be behind this. Demir was a high-priced professional who only operated in the most elite circles. Which meant only a select group would even know how to contact him, much less afford his price.

"Has he ever worked on American soil?" Eric asked.

"Nothing confirmed."

"I'll be back shortly. Let's keep this info between us for now."

Eric hung up, again stared at the face of the man in the pictures on his phone.

A Turkish assassin killing an American presidential candidate.

What the hell would they find next?

EIGHTEEN

April was tired of hiding out in her office all day. It had become exhausting keeping one eye on her laptop, pretending to work, while the other remained locked on her office door. She dreaded the possibility that her boss would walk in and confront her at any moment. She'd mentally practiced how she would react and what she'd say if it happened. *I have no idea what you're talking about, Mr. Sullivan. I didn't see anything on your phone. What is this all about?* Could she pull that off? She was never any good in theater and really didn't want to be put to the test. She thought about feigning illness and leaving work for the day. But then she was nervous that might also make her look suspicious. She kept trying to put the pieces together. Dean had texted her the information about Andrew Rainer, Senator Lambert's chief of staff. The firm didn't represent the Florida senator or any of his business interests, as far as she could tell. So what was the connection? Why was her boss exchanging cryptic text messages with his chief of staff?

Around midafternoon, April remembered Jerry Dawson's former legal secretary had abruptly left the firm right after his death. Sally Kimble was a quiet, pleasant woman who'd worked for the firm for many years. She was a good assistant. So why did she suddenly leave? Could it have had anything to do with Jerry and his now-mysterious boating death? April needed to talk with the woman. Sally's phone number was no longer active. But the head of HR was able to give April a physical address. Sally lived out in Marble Falls, about an hour west of Austin. April told her assistant she was leaving the office for a last-minute doctor's appointment. She then hit the sidewalk outside the building and began walking the three blocks south to her tenth-floor apartment in the Austonian.

The sidewalks were less busy than at lunch hour, so it was easier to keep an eye on those around her. She kept looking for the same guy from earlier. Tall, slender. Short, curly hair. Black windbreaker. So far, no sign of him. Had the guy actually been following her? Or was she just being paranoid? She quickly studied the other faces waiting at a crosswalk with her. A fortysomething woman wearing a gray business suit with her eyes locked on her cell phone. A sixtysomething couple in casual attire—jeans and T-shirts—who looked like they might be tourists. A squatty guy probably in his mid-thirties, buzz cut, goatee, camo-style jacket. Two men her age in business slacks, dress shirts, both wearing ties, who were chatting it up about golf.

When the walk sign appeared, they all collectively moved across together. April walked faster than the others. She crossed over Congress Avenue and approached the front of her high-rise apartment building. Another quick glance around her. Still no sign of Mr. Black Windbreaker. She felt somewhat relieved. This was all stressful enough without the additional fear of being followed. After pushing through the glass doors of her building, she paused one last time to take another look out to the sidewalk. She stiffened. The squatty guy in the camo jacket was standing on the sidewalk directly outside her entrance. The same guy with the buzz cut and goatee who'd been waiting at the crosswalk with her more than three blocks ago. Coincidence? She spun away, kept moving. Was this real? Was this guy also following her? Could he be working with the man in the black windbreaker? Did her boss send them?

April had no plans to go up to her apartment. Instead, she took the lobby elevator down into the underground parking garage, where her white BMW was in her designated spot. After starting it up, she pulled up to the exit on Second Street a moment later. April briefly paused at the exit, peered left to see if the guy was still standing outside the building. She cursed when she spotted him. This time, she lifted her phone and took a quick picture. Then she hit the gas before he noticed her and swiftly pulled away from the building.

April kept her eyes locked on her rearview mirror the entire drive outside of town. Was someone back there? Like a crazy driver, she kept speeding up and then slowing way down to watch what other cars on the highway did around her. Twice, she pulled over to the shoulder and acted like she was talking on her phone. As far as she could tell, she hadn't been followed by anyone. She finally reached the town of Marble Falls. After easing down some old farm roads, she spotted a one-story white farmhouse off by itself on several acres. An old pickup truck sat in the gravel driveway. Cows were in the field across the street. April pulled her BMW into the driveway behind the truck, got out, and approached the front door. She knocked, kept searching behind her. No black-windbreaker guy. No squatty guy. She thought she was safe.

A girl of four or five with incredibly cute reddish pigtails answered.

"Hi, are you Sally's daughter?" April asked.

The little girl eagerly nodded. "My name's Megan."

"I'm April. Is your mom here? I'm an old friend."

"You're pretty," she said, and then ran off into the house.

A moment later, Sally Kimble appeared from around the corner. She wore an apron over a blue sundress. April knew that Sally was in her late thirties and had four kids, ages four to eighteen. Her husband had been tragically killed in a trucking accident three years before April had joined the firm. The woman had displayed several pictures of her husband and the entire family on her desk back at the firm. With her husband gone, April figured Sally was the only source of income for her family. She had to be making good money at Michaels & Peterson.

Along with great benefits. So she again wondered why the woman would walk away from that kind of security.

"April?" she said, mouth widening. "What . . . what are you doing here?"

"Hi, Sally. I'm sorry to just show up like this. I tried to call, but you must have gotten a new phone number."

"No, it's fine. Just so surprised to see you."

They shared a quick hug.

"You have a beautiful place here," April mentioned.

"Thank you. It's my sister's land. Jack, my late husband, built this place by hand. Took him four years. We love it. That's why I never minded the long drive into town to go to work each day."

"Definitely more peaceful here than downtown."

Sally's brow wrinkled. "Is everything okay?"

April decided to get straight to the point. "I need to talk to you about Jerry."

This made Sally's face noticeably tighten. "Oh . . . okay."

"Do you have a minute?"

Sally stepped fully onto the front porch and shut the front door behind her.

"Why do you want to talk to me about Jerry?" she asked.

April had been pondering how to broach this topic on the way out. She'd finally decided the best approach was coming right out with it. Sally was no longer around the firm. So April didn't fear anything getting back to her boss.

"Something happened last night," April said. "Something bad. And I think Jerry was somehow involved."

"What do you mean?"

"Have you been watching the news?"

Sally looked away, shifted her weight uncomfortably. "We don't watch much TV out here. I like to keep the kids outdoors."

"But you know about the assassination?"

"Of course. My sister called me."

"It's about that."

April stayed quiet for a moment. She'd expected Sally to ask more about Jerry and why she'd mentioned the assassination. But she just let it be. Which April found unusually odd unless the woman already knew where this was going.

"Do you know why I'm here, Sally?"

Sally shook her head. "No. And I'm not sure I want to know."

"What do you mean by that?"

Sally exhaled slowly. "Listen, April. I appreciate you came all the way out here to see me. You are one of the few people I enjoyed being around at the firm. You've always been so sweet. But to be honest with you, I don't want to know why you're here. I don't want to know anything about the firm or about Jerry's past dealings. I was fond of Jerry. He wasn't perfect, but he was good to me. However, I left that world behind to take better care of my kids. And I don't want to be pulled back into it in any way."

April decided to press. "Did you quit the firm because you knew something illegal was going on there? Was Jerry a part of it?"

Sally didn't respond. She just stared down.

"What is it, Sally? Please, tell me."

Sally looked up again, eyes narrow. "Listen to me very carefully. You can't keep asking me these questions. I can't talk about it."

"Why? Do you not feel safe?"

Sally fidgeted. "April, please. You need to go."

"You can trust me, Sally. I promise. I need your help."

"Look, someone came to see me a month ago. He said he was a federal investigator. He was asking lots of questions about Jerry, about his legal dealings, about what I might know about them. I'm not sure I believe he worked for the government. He was very aggressive and threatening, claiming I could lose my kids if I didn't tell him the truth. I swore I didn't know anything. But he didn't seem to believe me. And then I noticed him following me around town for the next few days."

April wondered if it could've been one of the two guys who'd been following her today. "What did this guy look like?"

"Blond. Skinny. Probably a little older than you."

It wasn't one of her two guys. So who was it?

"It's had me scared, April," Sally said. "Which is why this conversation with you makes me very uncomfortable right now. I just want to be left alone."

"I'm scared, too, Sally," April admitted. "Two days ago, I discovered Jerry might have been involved with something that has put me in a dangerous position. I'm in real trouble, and I don't know what to do. That's why I'm here. I hoped you might know more. I'm sorry to have come here and upset you."

Sally told her to wait a moment. She went back inside and returned a couple of minutes later. She handed over a piece of notepad paper. April examined it. Sally had written down information about what looked like a storage facility. A unit number and all the necessary access codes.

"Nobody knows about this place," Sally said. "Jerry secretly kept some files here. I'm not sure why. But he had me set it up for him under my name a month before he died. I went there a couple of times. He asked me to tell no one about it."

"Am I looking for anything in particular?"

Sally nodded. "Lease Sale 151. That's all I can say, I'm sorry."

"I really appreciate this. Can we stay in touch?"

Sally gave her a phone number. April put it in her phone. And then she said goodbye and swiftly left, eager to find out what Jerry was hiding in storage.

NINETEEN

April spent an hour combing through a stack of banker boxes in Jerry Dawson's secret storage unit in South Austin before finally finding a thick folder labeled "Lease Sale 151." It was for a recent government auction involving blocks of land off the Gulf of Mexico for the sake of oil drilling. She sat down with the file at the closest coffee shop and began sifting through it. Lease Sale 151 had been scheduled to take place two months ago in New Orleans. The government was auctioning off 1.39 million acres of offshore oil blocks, 258 blocks in all. Each block to the highest bidder. Because drilling in the gulf was heavily restricted, the land was extremely valuable. It had not been touched in nearly twenty years. During that time, drilling technology had exploded. There was a lot of money to be made.

Eastwood Petroleum was the focus of the file. April had seen this name before, on Edward Sullivan's client list, but she'd never had any dealings with the company. The paperwork in the file showed that Sullivan was knee-deep on Eastwood's behalf with Lease Sale 151. However, Jerry's name was nowhere to be found. So April wondered why Jerry had a file on Eastwood Petroleum when they were Sullivan's client.

She grabbed her laptop and did a quick search on Eastwood. Their website said they were a private oil and natural gas company focused on the southern states, primarily Texas and New Mexico. With offices in Austin and Houston, the file listed them as pulling in revenues of $461 million last year. April returned to the file. Internal memos in the file suggested the company felt Lease Sale 151 was a good opportunity for them to expand operations. There were notepads with meeting dates going back more than a year out from the auction. The company decided to focus on several blocks, isolating Block 17, Block 33, Block 81, Block 94, and Block 111—each block a tract of nearly a hundred thousand acres. April sipped her coffee and sifted through more paperwork.

There were background documents on other government leases. A history of auctions. Maps detailing the gulf layout. Breakdowns of their most prominent competitors. A complete list of each competitor's leased property. Thick forecasts and analyses of what they expected from the competition, including emails back and forth between other lawyers representing other oil companies. Manuals describing the technical involvement of drilling offshore. And complete independent surveys of their designated blocks. They had clearly spent the big bucks necessary to be invested in this game and with this specific auction.

Government auctions like this involved blind bids in an effort to drive up the price to the absolute maximum value. Kind of like when multiple parties want to buy a house and get into a bidding war. Each party is instructed to make their best offer, and then the homeowner decides. If you really wanted the house, you'd better come in with your strongest offer, or you might lose it. However, most companies worked with their lawyers diligently behind the scenes in the months before to negotiate with each other, to settle pricing in advance—their best effort to keep prices down. There were usually very few surprises on auction day. April found nothing in the file about the results of the auction. The paperwork and notes led right up to the auction, but nothing afterward.

She again grabbed her laptop. She did a Google search for results on Lease Sale 151. The auction was held in New Orleans by the Minerals Management Service. She clicked on the first article she could find, a write-up from the New Orleans *Times-Picayune*. Twenty-seven companies took part in the bidding. They placed over 200 bids on 105 blocks for a total of over $500 million. April continued to search for an actual breakdown of Lease Sale 151. She finally found a list of bids, blocks, and winning companies. She scrolled down her screen, began matching up Eastwood's targets with their results. Everything matched up with their advanced negotiations. They had secured every block they'd wanted—except for one. Block 94. Instead, April found a company called J. Walter Petroleum. She stared at the name, wondered what had happened. There was no mention of J. Walter Petroleum in advanced negotiations. She searched the entire list of blocks. Block 94 was their only bid in the entire auction. They'd somehow secured it for $8 million.

April stared at the screen. Why had Eastwood let Block 94 go? It didn't make sense, according to the file. She had email exchanges in the file that said they'd agreed to spend $12 million in advanced negotiations with other firms to secure it. But they let it go for only $8 million. Why? She ran a search on J. Walter Petroleum. She found their poorly designed website and scanned a company profile. Based in Midland, Texas. Oil and gas exploration. Mainly West Texas. Small-time, to say the least. Barely a blip on the oil and gas exploration map. She read the names and profiles of the only two executives listed, didn't recognize either of them. According to more searching around, in the previous year, J. Walter had revenues of just over $7 million total. And somehow they'd just spent $8 million at Lease Sale 151?

Something didn't add up.

What had Jerry Dawson done?

TWENTY

Ben needed to make a quick stop at his apartment after work to grab some books before heading straight over to the library. He planned to study for a couple of hours and then meet up with Jenna for a late dinner. She was cramming as much as he was right now as they both tried to finish the school year strong. Ben had yet to tell his fiancée about what he'd discovered regarding his student loans. He'd called the registrar's office back a second time, to go over every single detail again, but he was told the exact same story. His college debt had been wiped out. The registrar did not usually turn down payment on student accounts, even if it came in under unusual circumstances.

Not that Ben wanted to reverse the event. He obviously wanted to believe there was a guardian angel out there who'd intentionally made the payment. At this point, Ben didn't know what else to do but celebrate with Jenna. So he'd made special reservations at her favorite restaurant and planned to surprise her with the incredible news.

Ben reached his apartment just as night was falling. He was surprised to find the front door cracked open. His roommate, Mike, had texted earlier to tell him he was driving up to Dallas for a job interview the next day. Had Mike not left yet? Ben opened the door, stood rigid in the entry for a moment. They had a small table just inside the door where they usually placed their keys and mail. Both slender drawers in the table were pulled all the way open. Ben noticed a stack of mail scattered on the floor at his feet. What the hell?

He stepped farther inside and stopped in the living room. He cursed, his eyes widening. The living room was a mess. And not just Mike's usual mess of opened pizza boxes and crumpled fast-food wrappers. The cushions were pulled off the sofa, the ottoman flipped upside down, the drawers of the media cabinet all pulled out. He peered into the kitchen. It looked the same as the living room. Cabinet doors left open, drawers pulled out, and papers scattered everywhere.

Ben whipped his head around when he thought he heard something coming from one of the two back bedrooms. "Mike?" he called out.

No response. Were they being robbed? Was the thief still here? Should he call the police? He heard another noise from the back. Someone was still in the apartment. Ben searched the kitchen, grabbed a small metal pan from the stovetop. Something to take a good crack at a person. He moved down the short hallway toward the bedrooms, paused in the middle, listened again. Both bedroom doors were currently shut, which was not unusual. Was the noise coming from his bedroom or his roommate's? He couldn't be sure. He put his hand on his own doorknob, took a quick breath, and pushed it open. He found no one staring back at him. But his bedroom was destroyed. Everything from his desk was tossed onto the carpet. His bathroom door was shut, but he could tell the light was on through the crack beneath it. Was someone inside?

He moved up to the door. His heart racing, he yanked open the bathroom door, ready to take a swing. But it was empty. Then he heard movement on the carpet behind him. Ben spun around. He saw someone zoom past his bedroom door in the hallway and head toward the living room. Looked like a guy in a gray sweatshirt with the hood over his head. Ben rushed forward, bolted out of his bedroom. The gray-hooded individual was already out the front door of his apartment. Ben raced toward the door and nearly slipped off his feet as he hit the second-story landing outside the unit. The thief was bounding down the stairwell three and four steps at a time.

"Hey!" Ben yelled, not really knowing what else to do.

The intruder did not look back. Ben started to chase but then stopped at the top of the stairs. The guy was already halfway across the parking lot. There was no way he was going to catch up with him. He was gone.

Ben went back inside his apartment, began searching through his messed-up things. Why would someone break into their apartment? He and Mike were two broke college students. They owned nothing valuable. Ben searched Mike's bedroom and found a similar disaster scene. Mike's items had also all been thrown about. But then Ben found something even more puzzling. Mike had left cash sitting out on top of his dresser. Ben picked it up, counted. Three hundred dollars. What the hell? The money was sitting out in the open. There was no way the thief hadn't seen it. If the gray-hooded guy was there to rob them, why hadn't he snatched it?

TWENTY-ONE

Eric was on the phone with the director, giving him the latest updates from the investigation, when Agent Brewster rushed into his office. It was clear by the look on the agent's face that he had something important to share. Eric held up a finger, finished his conversation, and hung up.

"What do you got?" he asked Brewster.

Brewster handed him a printout. "Take a look at this."

Eric scanned the paperwork. Someone's personal bank statement. He searched for a name at the top and found it. Theresa Barkley.

"Who is she?" Eric asked.

"Agent Barkley's wife."

Eric quickly put it together. Lamar Barkley was a young agent who had joined his team only six months ago. Quiet guy. Reserved. But he'd had no issues with him. Eric put a finger on the paperwork, searched, and found a circled entry.

He looked up at Brewster. "Fifteen thousand?"

"Cash deposit. Yesterday afternoon. We spoke with the bank teller a few minutes ago. She said Barkley made the deposit into his wife's account. She remembered it distinctly because they don't get a lot of cash deposits that size. She thought he was acting strange, too. Said he seemed jittery and kept glancing over his shoulder the entire time while he was standing at the counter."

Eric cursed. "Barkley was with Senator Carson the entire time."

"Right."

"What else do we know?"

"Barkley is in major debt. Stack of credit cards maxed out. Close to forty thousand bucks. His wife doesn't work, other than some part-time stuff at a preschool center. Three elementary-aged kids. Twin girls. And a boy. They are enrolled at an expensive private school. We talked to the school director. The Barkleys are overdue on the tuition payment."

"Barkley have money in the family?"

Brewster shook his head. "Doesn't look like it. Both he and his wife come from a modest background. No recent deaths or inheritance money we can find. She has a sister who is a nurse in Gainesville. His parents live in a two-bedroom condo in New Mexico. Father's a retired plumber. Barkley's brother is an electrician in Steubenville, Ohio. No trace of family money on either side."

"You run his cell phone and emails?"

"Yes, sir. We haven't found anything yet. Still digging."

"Where is Barkley?"

"Supposed to be working with Krieger's team tonight. But Krieger said he hasn't shown up or reported in."

Eric cursed again. He didn't like the sound of that. Could one of his own men have been the leak that got Carson killed?

"What about his wife?"

"She's at home with the kids. We have two agents waiting in a car outside. Just didn't want to send them in until I got the go-ahead from you."

"Good. Let's go talk to Mrs. Barkley. Hopefully this is nothing."

Agent Cutler, one of the two men at Barkley's house, met them on the front sidewalk and updated Eric on the situation. Barkley was gone.

His wife said he'd gone out for an afternoon jog on the running trail near their house and hadn't returned. It had already been four hours. She was worried. She'd searched the trail herself an hour ago but found nothing. His car was still parked in the driveway. He hadn't taken any personal things with him. No phone. No clothes. No toiletries. Not even his wallet. She said he'd been acting strange the past two days. Edgy and temperamental. But he claimed it was just stress from work. His wife admitted she was concerned her husband had started gambling again. She said Barkley'd had real problems with sports betting a couple of years ago. Got them into enough trouble where they had to sell their first house and live in a tiny apartment for a year until they recovered. Theresa was shocked at the mention of a $15,000 cash deposit. She claimed she knew nothing about it. She had no idea where the money came from. They believed her.

"We searching the trail?" Eric asked the agent.

"Yes, sir. Wilson is out there right now." Cutler's phone buzzed, and he looked at the screen. "Hold up. That's him now."

Cutler answered, listened, and then cursed. "Send us a map pin. Be there in a second."

Cutler hung up, said, "Found him. It ain't good."

Eric felt his heart sink. "Dead?"

Cutler nodded. "Shot in the head."

"Self-inflicted?" Brewster asked.

"Nope. Kill shot in the back of the head. Dragged into the bushes."

Eric exhaled heavily, ran both hands over his bald head, feeling the weight of that news. One of his own guys had betrayed them. That seemed pretty clear. And now he was dead because of it, leaving behind a wife and three small children. It was a devastating blow, both professionally and personally.

"Get our crime scene unit over there," Eric instructed.

"Yes, sir," Cutler replied.

"I'll go talk to the wife."

TWENTY-TWO

After returning to the office, April put in a few more overly anxious hours before finally leaving with a few other associates around eight that evening. That was early for her, but she wasn't sure how much longer she could keep doing this. Sitting there and chewing off her fingernails. Avoiding her boss. Pretending like nothing was going on when every stone she turned over told her otherwise. She envied her colleagues right now. They kept yapping away about nonsense, talking about hitting up the bars after work, without much care in the world other than their own billing sheets.

That was her life forty-eight hours ago.

And then a bomb was dropped in her lap.

She climbed into her BMW in the office parking garage and drove out of downtown proper. She again kept her eyes glued to her rearview mirror, wondering if she was being followed. She had not spotted anyone upon returning to work earlier that evening. After ten minutes of driving around, April pulled her car into a parking lot outside of Barton Creek Square, a shopping mall that sat up on a hill overlooking the city, and found an open spot outside the Nordstrom department store. She sat there a second, again checking her surroundings, watching as different people got in and out of their cars. She thought of the faces of the two men she believed had been following her earlier in the day. She was growing more paranoid by the minute. Her visit with Sally Kimble had not helped ease those feelings. April had called Sally to ask a few follow-up questions. The woman was still hesitant but seemed to be warming up to becoming more involved. She knew more, April could tell. It seemed like Jerry Dawson had done something in secret before his death—if he was indeed dead. But was Lease Sale 151 connected to it? And was Jerry's death somehow connected to the assassination of Senator Carson?

April grabbed her workbag, got out of her car, and walked toward the entrance to Nordstrom. Her eyes bounced around everywhere. Was she in the clear? She entered the department store and briskly paced the aisles. Nordstrom was busy as usual, as the city's affluent citizens stuffed designer bags full of the latest fashions. But she was not there to shop. She had other plans. She checked her watch. She needed to kill some time. She'd intentionally come early to make sure she wasn't being followed.

She found the entrance to the main corridor, entered, and scanned the stores around her. She walked a little way and then ducked into a lingerie store. She circled a rack of negligees and peered out the front window, where she watched for any signs of being followed. Nothing. She stalled for five minutes, aimlessly pushing underwear items around a rack, and then left the store and moved farther down the corridor. She slipped inside a baby-clothes shop, again watching the windows and the walkers. After hanging inside the store a few minutes, she left and got lost deeper in the mall.

There was still no sign of her two pals.

April hit an escalator, ascended to the second level, and paused to look over a railing below her. Still good. She ducked away inside the Gap, where she purchased a blue V-neck sweater, some blue jeans, a pair of brown tennis shoes, and a red ball cap. She found the changing room, undressed, put on her new clothing, and stuffed her business outfit and heels into her shopping bag. She then tucked her brown hair up beneath the back of her red ball cap and pulled the brim down to hide her eyes.

Ms. Anonymous.

She moved back into the corridor and continued to work her way down the huge mall. She paused at every mall sign and directory, constantly checking behind her. She walked fast and then slow, and then she'd spin around and suddenly rush off in the opposite direction. She was starting to get good at this. But that didn't sit well. She didn't want to get good at this. She just wanted this to be over. She wanted her life back. But she had a bad feeling her life might never be normal again.

She bought a cup of coffee at a small café, then hid at a table along the railing near the food court, where she had a view of both the second floor and the level below. She snuggled up closely to the railing, her eyes hidden behind the coffee cup. Then she saw them. Both of them. And it made her chest tighten. She couldn't believe it. The taller one in the black windbreaker with the short, curly hair. The squattier one with the goatee and camo jacket. The odd couple. Oscar and Felix. They were working together. The two men were on the lower level, intently watching shoppers, whispering among themselves. How did they know she was here at the mall? Could they be tracking her phone? Her car? She could feel her heart pounding inside her chest.

For a moment, she wondered if she should abort her plans. But she decided against that. The two men knew she was inside the mall. But they clearly didn't know where she was right now. All her darting around, hiding in retail shops, and changing clothes had worked. When they peered up in her direction, April ducked away before cautiously looking back. They didn't notice her. They weren't looking for the blue sweater and red ball cap. They were looking for the lawyer. April grabbed both her workbag and shopping bag, abandoned her coffee, and quickly left her perch.

TWENTY-THREE

Dean walked through the shopping mall, hands in jacket pockets, feeling lost already. He searched the mall directory. He didn't know his way around the huge place. He rarely shopped, as evidenced by his clothes—mostly T-shirts and blue jeans. He found where he needed to go on the mall map, took a right. The mall was busy. Shoppers were in full swing. Half of them looked like teenagers. He located an escalator and headed up. Nordstrom was ahead. He glanced at his watch. Right on time. He entered the department store, searched the store signs, followed the aisles. It looked like all women's clothes on the second level of the store. He asked a store attendant for the dressing rooms, explained he was searching for his wife. She guided him over to the corner. As expected, he found April waiting for him inside one of the small private changing rooms. They huddled closely together. He tried not to think about how good she smelled.

"Nice ball cap," he said, studying her outfit.

"Thanks. It was necessary."

"Everything okay?"

"No, they're out there, Dean. I saw them."

He cursed. "You sure?"

"Definitely. Oscar and Felix. Both of them."

"Oscar and Felix?"

"You're not the only one who can come up with nicknames."

Dean had mentioned Andrew Rainer as the "professor" a couple of times. April had described the two men to him earlier and even sent him a text photo of the short, squatty fellow in the camo jacket.

"You think they followed you from the office?" he asked.

"I'm not sure how. I was driving like a crazy idiot."

"They're tracking you somehow."

"I lost them for now. But let's be quick, just in case."

"Yeah, okay."

Dean pulled out a cell phone from his left jacket pocket. It was a prepaid burner phone he'd purchased at Target twenty minutes ago. "Use this from now on to communicate with me. I don't want to take any more chances."

"Good idea." She placed it in her workbag. "Did you find out anything more on Andrew Rainer?"

"Not much. Harvey says Senator Lambert and Carson have been known enemies for a long time now. Obviously, Carson beat out Lambert for the party nomination earlier this year. We all know that was ugly as hell."

"Still, enemies enough for Lambert to be involved in Carson's death?"

"Doubtful. That was just normal politics."

"Right. And it doesn't explain why my boss is involved."

"Harvey and I are still digging. What did Sally Kimble say?"

She told him all about her uneasy conversation with Sally, the secret storage unit rented by his father, the file on mysterious Lease Sale 151, and the inexplicable results of the offshore oil auction a couple of months ago. Reaching into her workbag, she pulled out the thick file and handed it over to him.

"I wonder why my father had this," Dean said.

"Your dad got involved somehow. Sally pointed me here for a reason. J. Walter Petroleum is a nobody company up in Midland. It makes zero sense how they won this block of land. Something happened that helped them pull it off."

"Do you think Sally would talk directly to me?"

"Maybe. I don't want to push her too hard, but she clearly knows more than she's saying. She's just scared. Can't blame her."

"I may reach out. And I'll start my own research on this Midland company."

April ran her fingers through her hair. Dean noticed her hands were trembling. He reached over, took one of them in his own hand. "Hey, are you okay?"

She shook her head. "No, but does it matter?"

"Yes, it matters. You don't have to keep doing this. You don't owe it to anyone. I can go talk to my brother. And you could get on a plane tonight and just leave town. Tell the firm you have a family emergency. Let the smoke clear. I'll take it from here."

"No, I need to see this through."

"Why?"

"Because my boss might be a killer, Dean. Or at least a willing participant in some kind of killing operation. I have no future with the firm until I figure that out. And the only way for us to do that is probably from the inside."

He exhaled. He still didn't like it. And a big part of him wanted to talk to Eric about this without April knowing about it. If it came down to it, he would protect her even if she was unwilling to protect herself.

"Just promise me you're being careful with every step."

"You think I'm wearing this stupid red ball cap, this sweater, these brown shoes, and meeting you in a department-store dressing room just for the fun of it?"

"Okay, I hear you."

She gave him a brief smile, squeezed his hand back. "We should go."

"Keep the new phone I gave you handy at all times."

Dean left the changing room first. He moved all the way across the second level of the department store and turned back to watch. He scanned the crowd. No sign of her odd couple: Oscar and Felix. Who were they? April left the changing room a few minutes later. The red cap's brim was pulled way down on her forehead. And only a few strands of hair poked out the back. With her bags in hand, she walked purposely down a few aisles and found an escalator in the middle of the store. Dean watched everyone on the second level. He wasn't going to limit his search to just the two men. There could be others. But he didn't spot anyone who looked suspicious. When April disappeared down the escalator, he moved in behind her, trailed at a safe distance. She reached the first floor and quickly headed toward an exit. She was out the glass doors a moment later. Dean monitored her all the way through the parking lot. He watched her climb inside her BMW and then zip away. He kept his eyes on the parking lot and saw no other cars in pursuit.

TWENTY-FOUR

After leaving the mall, Dean picked up his two nephews from flag football practice a half hour later after Eric sent him an urgent text message begging for his help. He then took them over to Amy's Ice Cream, loaded them up on sugar, and watched them run around throwing a football on a grass lawn. The oldest, Grayson, had some good ball skills. For a skinny kid, he could throw the football far—just like his Uncle Dean, who had played quarterback all the way through his sophomore year at TCU before tearing up his shoulder and ending his sports career.

Eric finally arrived, looking out of breath and exhausted. He sat on a bench next to Dean and watched the boys play together.

"I really appreciate you doing this," Eric said. "There was no way I was going to call Tina and ask her to go get them. She'd have thrown it right back in my face. She's not offering me much grace these days."

"I'm always happy to do it."

"I'll pay you back for the ice cream."

"Don't worry about it. How're you holding up? You look wiped out."

"I am." Eric sighed. "Haven't slept since I last saw you. And I got hit square in the chest by some devastating news a few hours ago."

"What happened?"

Eric looked over. "Off the record?"

"Sure."

"Probably shouldn't tell you this, because I'm still not sure how we're going to handle it all. But I just found out one of my own guys leaked the information about which exact vehicle Carson was riding in last night."

"You're kidding?"

"I wish. Got paid fifteen thousand in cash for it. And that's not all. Someone shot him dead this afternoon."

"Damn, Eric. That's awful."

"Yeah, I'm sick about it. I got one guy fighting for his life in the hospital, and now another one is dead."

"I'm sorry, man. No wonder you look like hell."

The news hit Dean harder than he let on. He'd had every intention to talk to his brother tonight about April's situation. Even if she became furious with him about it. This was way too dangerous. He didn't want to risk her safety anymore. But now he wasn't sure what to do. While he trusted his brother, he no longer believed the FBI could keep her safe. Not if one of their own agents was directly involved in the death of Carson. How could he put April into their hands? He suddenly felt out on his own again.

"You still think the Zeta Cartel is behind all of this?" Dean asked.

"No. We'll likely put that news out tomorrow."

"Can I publish it tonight?"

"Only if you want to get your ass beat by your big brother."

"If not them, then who?"

"The suspect list is still too long for my taste."

"Who's on it? Any politicians?"

Eric cocked his head. "Like who?"

Dean shrugged. "Just asking. It's got to be politically motivated, right?"

Eric's eyes narrowed. "Do you know something I don't know?"

Dean really wanted to bring up the possibility of Senator Lambert being involved, but he couldn't figure out a way to do it without pulling

April directly into the conversation. And there was no way he was going to do that now. He felt handcuffed.

"No. Just digging for information."

Eric was quiet, studying him for a moment. It was clear he didn't necessarily believe Dean. "If you know anything about what's going on, Dean, share it. This is not the time to play your reporter games with me."

"I'm not playing games. I'm just doing my job."

"Your job is writing words. My job is life and death. They're not equal."

"I understand that."

Dean wanted to say his job felt like life and death at the moment. But he didn't want to get into it right now. Not until he figured out what to do next.

Eric rolled his head around his neck. "You're a stubborn ass."

"Learned it from you."

Eric grinned. "Probably true."

They quietly watched the boys running around for another minute.

"Will looks more like Dad every day," Dean mentioned.

"Yeah. Tina hates that."

"I've been thinking about him a lot lately."

Eric looked over. "Who? Dad?"

"Yeah."

"Why?"

"Just been on my mind the past couple of days. Do you remember your last conversation with Dad?"

"Yeah. Wasn't a good one. I chewed him out for missing Will's birthday party after he promised he'd be there."

"I remember that. Will was bummed."

"Will forgot all about it the next day when Dad sent the giant LEGO Star Wars set. That was Dad, though, you know. He thought money was the answer to everything. And he always thought he could buy our affection back with big gifts. Sure, it might have given us momentary happiness as kids, but it never lasted."

"Yeah, we only wanted him and not his money. But that was never good enough for Dad. He was obsessed with making money. He recklessly spent everything he had on stupid stuff like that ridiculous Ferrari and the huge penthouse apartment. Why would he ever need six thousand square feet spread over two floors?"

"I think it was because of his poor upbringing."

"Maybe," Dean said. "My last conversation was Dad swearing to me he'd given up drinking for good. He claimed to be sixty-two days sober. Which is why it's been hard for me to make peace with what happened on that boat."

"You believed him?"

"I wanted to believe it."

"Mom told us the same thing every three months growing up. But nothing ever changed. The nature of the disease."

"I know . . . it's just . . . did you notice a change in Dad before he died?"

"Maybe. But I probably had too many defense mechanisms built up over the years to ever allow myself to fully believe anything he said to me."

"Understandable. You always took the brunt of it for me and Ben."

"It's weird you're bringing up Dad tonight."

"Why?"

"Ben called me this afternoon. He said some woman came to the pub today while he was working and started asking him all about Dad. He said it was bizarre."

"Bizarre how?"

"She wanted to know if he'd talked with Dad *recently*. He kept reminding her Dad was dead, but she couldn't seem to get her mind around it."

"Who was she?"

"Ben wasn't sure. She never identified herself."

Bringing up the possibility that their father might still be alive was something Dean also wanted to do tonight—after he told Eric about

April's involvement. If it was true, Eric might have the resources to track their father down. The thought had invigorated him. But he'd squashed this idea after finding out about the FBI leak. He had to keep April out of this. And he couldn't bring up their dad without exposing her in the process.

Dean thought about what Eric had just told him. Who was this woman who'd visited Ben? Could she know something about the mystery around the boating accident? He needed to speak with Ben and find out more about this conversation. The challenge was, Ben still didn't want to speak with him. He'd tried calling him several times over the past few weeks to work things out, but Ben was still upset about him skipping the funeral. He'd always been close to Ben, so it had sucked having the fracture between them. He knew his little brother would get over it eventually. But he now had an even more compelling reason to get the dialogue going between them again.

He pulled out his phone, sent his younger brother a quick text.

Can we please talk?

TWENTY-FIVE

The next morning, Dean caught an early flight out of Austin and flew into the tiny Midland Airport. He decided he wanted to have this conversation in person and not over the phone. Hank Starch was head of J. Walter Petroleum, a company of only seven full-time employees, according to a brief company profile he'd found online. It was easy for him to get an appointment when Dean said he was doing a story on promising small oil companies. Hank Starch was eager to make room for him in his schedule.

Dean took a quick Uber drive to a nondescript redbrick building sitting next to an Arby's restaurant. It was certainly not a glamorous company headquarters. They met in Hank's office. He was a short man of sixty or so, with curly white hair and an amiable face. He wore a gray Western-style sport coat, blue jeans, a belt buckle, and black cowboy boots. The picture of a West Texas oilman. He spent the first twenty minutes telling Dean all about the history of the company. Dean finally managed to steer the conversation around to the reason he was there.

"Tell me about New Orleans and Lease Sale 151."

Hank grinned. "Yes, the day the Good Lord smiled down on us. That auction was a very big step for us. Securing that tract in the gulf is our first step to expanding and competing on a more prominent level."

"Your investors have already seen a quick return."

"And it's just going to get better. Everybody around here is expecting an enormous boost with this new offshore project. We've had more investors approach us. That's why you see so many smiling faces when you walk these hallways. It's exciting for us. We feel like we finally put on our big-boy pants."

"What made you get involved in the auction? I reviewed your records. You'd never participated in anything like that. Most of what you do is out here in West Texas."

"That's true. We really know the land here. We already have the relationships that we've built over the decades. But we just felt it was time to expand. Our investors agreed."

Dean studied the man in front of him. So far, there was nothing peculiar about what he was sharing. "Hank, I have to be honest. I'm surprised you were willing to risk so much financially. Just doing the research for that block must have cost you hundreds of thousands of dollars, if not more than that. That's a lot of money for a company like yours, without any guarantee of return on that investment. I've interviewed companies that spent millions just in research and surveys alone before ever bidding on the land."

"You're right. It was a risk."

Hank left it at that.

"Why did you choose Block 94?"

"Great research. It fell right into our sweet spot. Small enough to be ignored by the bigger players. But still had a ton of potential."

"There was at least one other much larger company that wanted that property. My sources say they negotiated in advance to secure it, which is how I know most of these deals go down. You weren't in those negotiations. Your last-second bid and victory surprised everyone. What happened?"

Hank chuckled. "We snuck down there like a rattlesnake and bit them in the ass."

"Right." Dean was tired of the clichés. "But what's the real story?"

Hank pressed his lips together. "I'm not sure what you're suggesting."

"It's suspicious, Hank. That's all I'm saying."

"Are you implying we did something illegal?"

"I'm just saying, from an outsider's perspective, it makes no sense."

"It made plenty sense to us, son." Hard lines formed in Hank's forehead. They did a staring match for a moment. "Why are you really here, Dean?"

"I'll shoot straight with you. I know for a fact there is more to what happened in New Orleans with Block 94. That's the real story I'm working on. And I intend to flip over every rock from here to New Orleans until I find the answers. I'm here because I wanted to give you a shot to give me your version of the story before I publish. Do you know a man named Jerry Dawson?"

"Never heard of him."

Hank's eyes didn't even twitch. Dean believed him.

Hank leaned forward on his desk. "When are you going to publish this?"

"Tomorrow," Dean lied, trying to compel the man to tell the truth. "It will be up on our website first thing. It's going to shine a real spotlight on you. So I hope everything you're telling me checks out."

Hank sighed, put his hands together in front of him. He stared out his window for a moment before returning his attention to Dean.

"Any chance we can talk off the record?" he said.

"Sure."

"If I tell you this, Dean, I need you to promise to keep us out of your story. We all have families and kids to take care of around here. As you can see, we're not some big corporation. We can't handle a scandal. It might crush us."

"I'm not out to get you, Hank. I promise. But I believe there is a much bigger story at play here than what has happened with your company."

Hank looked down at his hands, smiled slightly as his mind drifted. "It's a fascinating tale. I honestly still don't know what to make of it."

He told his story. A few months before the auction—an auction that was nowhere near their radar at the time—his partner, Chuck, received an anonymous phone call. The man on the phone started talking about Lease Sale 151, coming up in New Orleans, and suggested they get involved. The man wouldn't give his name, but Chuck figured based off the man's use of their terminology, he was familiar with their business. Chuck assured the man that J. Walter Petroleum was not interested. But the man on the phone asked if they'd be interested if he could provide the research and guarantee successful results.

So Chuck called Hank into his office, told him what was going on, and Hank got on the phone with this stranger. Again, the man wouldn't identify himself. But he gave Hank the same spiel he'd just given to Chuck. Both Chuck and Hank thought the guy was nuts, but he knew so much about the auction that they were intrigued. So the next day, the man overnighted them a package of information, with instructions to call a phone number if they were interested. There were also instructions to not tell a living soul about their interaction or the deal was off. Real secretive and all.

"He never identified himself?" Dean asked.

"Not once. And we didn't take him too seriously until we got the package."

"What was in it?"

Hank shook his head. "Just about everything we could ever want to know about Block 94. Charts, graphs, everything. Someone, or some company, had done a ton of research, spent millions, and I'm guessing this guy stole it from another company. We looked it over and got really interested. But then after making a few phone calls, we discovered another much bigger company, as you suggested, had their sights set on Block 94, among others."

"What did you do?"

"Tossed the package in the corner. Forgot about it. We knew we couldn't negotiate with these players. It was way out of our league. But this guy was persistent. He called us back, told us to not be concerned with the other company, that he had that end covered. And then he went on to tell us exactly how the auction would play out, with us submitting our bid and coming away with a win."

"Did you believe him?"

"Of course not. It was ridiculous. But at the same time, Chuck and I got to wondering. What if it was real? What if the guy really could somehow work the system? We could slip under the radar and grab it. Don't get me wrong, it would still take a bunch of money, more than we'd ever paid for any property, but the potential reward would far outweigh any risk."

"You had the eight million?"

"Heck no. We set up a few meetings. Squeezed out as much as possible by telling our investors as little as possible. But we were only able to come up with four million."

"And you knew that wouldn't be enough."

"Yeah, we knew we needed at least twice that. Which leads to the second part of our little fairy tale. That afternoon, while we're scratching our heads about only pulling together four million, we got a visit from a potential investor. Someone we've never met before. She just showed up here at our office. A wealthy widow. She decided to fly out to see us in person. Real mysterious. She said her lawyers had done their research and she wanted to invest in our company."

"Four million dollars."

Hank smiled, shaking his head. "Bingo."

"What was her name?"

"Ms. Ida Jo Welsher. She had the money and was willing to wire it that afternoon. But she also had a special contract drawn up by her attorneys. If she invested the four million now, every year for the next four years, we would be required to wire her five million in return."

Dean whistled. "Twenty million dollars total?"

"Yep. She was an interesting lady, let me tell you. But the thing is, if everything went according to what we were promised at that auction, we knew our little company had the potential to explode over the next few years. We'd begun doing our own research. And we realized that twenty million was not at all unreasonable. Unusual, yes. Unconventional, certainly. But not unrealistic. Especially if that's what it took to buy our way into the auction."

"Did she ever mention Lease Sale 151?"

"Not once. As if that sweet woman had no idea what was going on. But get this. The legal contract stipulated that we had the right to return the money within ninety days if we changed our mind."

Dean did the math. "Ninety days would put you on the other side of the auction."

Hank nodded. "Exactly. Basically, the mastermind behind all of this was lending us the money to get into an auction he was going to somehow manipulate. That's how much confidence he had that everything would turn out the way he'd promised. We could give the money back and tear up the contract if it didn't work."

"So you made the agreement?"

"Of course. Chuck and I figured, why the hell not. Let's just play dumb and move forward. Being ignorant is not illegal. So we signed the papers. We decided we had nothing to lose. Maybe some time, a trip to New Orleans, but that was it. And we had absolutely everything to gain."

Dean was mesmerized. "What happened in New Orleans?"

"Everything happened exactly as the mystery man suggested. We made a last-minute bid, out of nowhere, and won the block."

"You mean you won the lottery."

"We won the lottery," Hank agreed.

"Did you ever hear back from either of them? The man? Or Ms. Welsher?"

"Never. Of course, we haven't exactly gone looking for them, either."

Dean stared out the window, thought about his father. He was clearly the man he'd made the arrangement with for the auction. But who was the woman? Who was Ida Jo Welsher?

"What did the woman look like?"

"Mid-forties. Striking blond hair. Attractive."

Dean ruled out his initial thought of Sally Kimble. Could it have been the same woman who'd visited Ben at the pub yesterday? His younger brother still hadn't returned his text message requesting to talk.

Hank said, "We did hear from some other men. A couple of guys show up real quick after the auction, asking us a lot of questions. Wearing suits. Flashing badges. Said they were with some special government investigative unit. We didn't believe that. Chuck and I made an agreement behind closed doors to never talk about it again. Not in the office. Not to our wives, our kids, to anyone, anywhere. We got rid of the research, got drunk, had a bonfire in the middle of a cattle field, and haven't said a thing to each other ever since."

"And no one has come back around?"

"Not until yesterday."

"Someone came to see you yesterday?"

"Yeah. But this guy was different. Not a suit with a fake badge. But a menacing-looking guy wearing a black leather jacket. Claimed to be a private investigator. Asked the same type of questions. I told him I knew nothing. But he didn't leave it at that. He started making threats about my safety. And he then began telling me details about my family, my grandkids, saying it would be a shame if one of them got hurt because their granddad wasn't being truthful. Struck the fear of God in me, to be honest."

"You tell Chuck?"

"Not yet. Chuck recently had a hospital stay for a heart issue. He's still recovering. I didn't want to chance scaring him to death. Been wrestling like hell with what to do about it. Might go to the police, but I didn't want to do it without Chuck knowing. I know I need to tell someone about it in case something happens to me. I guess that someone is you, Dean. I don't know what kind of story you're working on, or who all it involves, but I do know one thing. What happened down there in New Orleans was one of the strangest things I've ever seen in my life. Someone played puppet master against powerful companies with hundreds of millions on the line. I'd be very careful if I were you."

TWENTY-SIX

April intentionally left her cell phone in the bottom drawer of her desk, slipped out of the office without telling anyone, and caught a taxi around the corner from her building. She had growing concerns that her phone and maybe even her car were being tracked. She had no other way of explaining how her two followers had unexpectedly shown up at the mall last night. She wouldn't take any more chances. While she didn't spot Oscar or Felix when she arrived at work this morning, she knew that didn't necessarily mean anything. They could still be back there somewhere. For extra precaution, she had the first taxi drop her six blocks away from her pickup point and then immediately grabbed a second taxi to continue her journey. Ten minutes later, she got out and stood in front of Ben's apartment building. Because Dean's younger brother didn't seem too keen on responding to his text invite to talk, April decided to pay her own visit. They needed answers. They needed to know more about the woman who came to see Ben yesterday. She might be someone of importance in their investigation. April climbed the apartment stairs and knocked on his second-story door. A guy answered wearing sweatpants and a black tank top.

"Is Ben around?" she asked.

"No, he's over at the bar where he works."

April peered around him and noticed the apartment looked like a disaster zone. "You his roommate?"

"Yeah, I'm Mike."

"I'm April. I'm a friend of his brother Dean."

"Oh, yeah. I've met Dean. Cool guy." He seemed to notice her wandering eyes. "I promise we're not usually this messy. Someone broke into our apartment last night and destroyed the place. I'm trying to get everything picked up."

"Sorry to hear that. You guys okay?"

"Yeah, we're fine. I wasn't here. Ben actually walked in on it. But he's good. He ran the guy off. Crazy thing is, the dude didn't even steal anything."

"He broke in and didn't take anything?"

"Yeah. Weird, right?"

April tilted her head. First, a strange woman visited Ben, asking about his father. Then his apartment got broken into by someone. The two incidents had to be related.

"Crown & Anchor, right?" she asked.

"Yep. You know where it is?"

"I do, thanks."

A few minutes later, April found Ben behind the bar at the pub. She'd been around Ben quite a lot while she was with Dean and had always enjoyed his company. He was a good-hearted person with an easygoing laugh. They had common ground because of her profession and would often swap law school horror stories. His fiancée, Jenna, was also fun to be around. She'd missed hanging out with them. That was the hard thing about breakups. You lose more than just the person you've been dating.

"Hey, Ben," she said, approaching him.

He glanced up from the bar, cocked his head. "April?"

She smiled. "Hi, how are you?"

"Uh, good . . . What're you doing here?"

"I need to speak with you for a moment."

"What's up?"

"In private," she suggested.

"Yeah, sure. I could use the break."

They found a quiet table in the corner and sat on opposite sides.

"Gosh, it feels like forever since I've seen you," he said.

"Your dad's funeral."

"Right. That day was a blur. Why do you need to speak with me?"

"It's actually about your father, Ben."

"Oh, okay. What about him?"

"I guess you told Eric a strange woman came to see you here yesterday and was asking all about your dad?"

"How did you know that?"

"Eric told Dean. Dean told me."

"Wait . . . are you two back together?"

"Not exactly. Dean and I are working together on something. He wanted me to come talk to you since you're not responding to him."

"Oh . . . yeah, he sent me a text yesterday. I haven't replied yet. Sorry if that caused you to come all the way over here to find me. Just stupid brother stuff."

"No problem. It's good to see you. You should know Dean regrets not going to the funeral. He said that's why you've been angry at him. I hate to see you guys like this. You've always been so close."

"I should probably get over it. So, what about my father?"

"I'm in a bad situation at the firm."

"What's going on?"

April gave a quick glance around, looking for any wandering eyes—a necessary habit she'd formed over the past two stressful days—and then leaned in even closer. "I recently found out your dad was involved in something troubling before he died. And I'm wondering if this woman who came to see you had something to do with it."

"Really?"

"Can you tell me about your conversation?"

"I mean, I don't know what to say, April. She was acting weird. She seemed distraught. I could tell she'd been crying. Her eyes were bloodshot. She kept asking me if I'd spoken with my dad recently. She wasn't making any sense."

"She didn't give you her name?"

He shook his head. "But she left me a phone number. Asked me to call her if I hear anything about my dad. Whatever that means."

"Do you still have the phone number?"

"Yeah, give me a second."

He got up, walked back over to the bar, found his backpack, rummaged through it, and then returned to their table. He set a piece of notepad paper in front of her. April took a photo of it on her new burner phone.

"What's going on, April?" Ben asked. "Did my dad do something illegal?"

"I don't know. There's some mystery around your dad's final days. We discovered a case he was working on with a client that wasn't his. Case worth millions that went sideways." She didn't want to go into much detail. It was best if Ben didn't know more than necessary. For his own protection. "What else can you tell me about this woman? What did she look like?"

"She was probably mid- to late forties. A very attractive blond woman. Nicely dressed. Rich, based off her clothes and jewelry. She had the biggest dang diamond wedding ring I've ever seen. I notice these things now."

April considered this information. It was the exact same description Hank Starch had given to Dean this morning about the mystery woman who showed up out of nowhere to unexpectedly invest four million dollars into J. Walter Petroleum a few months ago. Ida Jo Welsher. A name that brought up zero results in an online search.

"And that's all she said and left?" she asked.

"Yeah, that's it. So bizarre. But then it's been a strange twenty-four hours for me all the way around."

"I talked to your roommate. I heard about the break-in last night."

"He tell you the guy didn't even steal anything?"

"He did."

"And that's not even the weirdest thing that's happened lately. Someone claiming to be my uncle paid off over a hundred thousand dollars of my student debt this past week."

"Wow. I didn't know you guys had an uncle."

"That's the thing, April. We don't. The money came from an account in the Cayman Islands. I've called the institution but can't get any more information."

April immediately flashed on the original text exchange between Edward Sullivan and Andrew Rainer. *Dawson still hasn't broken. He's a tough SOB*. If Dean's father were still alive, could he be living abroad? Could he have been the one who'd paid off Ben's student debt? Did this mysterious blond woman know the truth about him?

April glanced over to the bar. "Does the pub have security cameras?"

"Yes."

"Can we look at the footage of the woman from yesterday?"

"Probably. Let me find out."

April followed Ben down a hallway to a back office. He had a quick conversation with an older guy who appeared to be the pub manager. Seconds later, they were sitting down in front of a computer while Ben scrolled through yesterday's security footage. The security camera was stationed behind the bar and showed a clear image of Ben's back while he was cleaning glasses with a hand towel. A moment later, a woman who matched the description Ben had given earlier entered and sat on a stool. Mid-forties. Attractive. Blond hair. Well dressed. April immediately recognized her. She couldn't believe her eyes. Trisha Sullivan. Her boss's wife. What the hell? She watched the entire encounter but didn't mention to Ben she knew the woman. Her brain was firing in a dozen different directions. Trisha Sullivan and Jerry Dawson obviously knew each other. Jerry and her boss were longtime partners. She had to be the same woman who'd visited Hank Starch in Midland. Were she and

Jerry working together? Or was it something else? Had Sullivan sent her to Ben yesterday to ask questions?

After thanking Ben and leaving the pub, April pulled out her burner phone in the parking lot and immediately called the phone number the woman had left behind. April had been around Trisha probably a half dozen times at various law firm functions over the past two years. She always seemed sharp and well put together. In her past life, she'd been a successful marketing executive. But she'd walked away from that world when she married Edward Sullivan a few years ago. The phone rang four times and then went to an automated voicemail without a personalized greeting. April wondered if it could be a burner phone just like hers. April was hesitant to identify herself, just in case the woman was acting on behalf of her boss. But she had to take a risk. The clock was ticking. And her gut said Sullivan had no idea what his wife was doing. April gave her name, said she was calling about Jerry Dawson and it was urgent, and asked for a return call.

TWENTY-SEVEN

Matamoras, Mexico.

A football toss across the Texas border near Brownsville, the very southern tip of the United States. Eric huddled in a black Suburban with Special Agent Rick Bosa, the head of the Brownsville FBI office, and a Mexican federal agent named Alberto Mendoza. A Texas-Mexico border surveillance video had made a potential identification of the assassin, Yusuf Demir. Eric had watched it himself and agreed there were strong possibilities. When the license plate on the man's car identified it as stolen in Austin yesterday, Eric made the trip to South Texas.

Four more FBI agents were sitting in another unmarked SUV behind them, all of them staring at a dingy Mexican motel with chickens roaming around in the dirt parking lot. The place was a dump. However, if you were an assassin perhaps waiting to strike again but not wanting to be tracked in the United States, this would not be a bad hideout. You could be in Houston within a few hours. From there, you could go anywhere in the world on a direct flight.

"What do we know, Mendoza?" Eric asked the Mexican agent. He was a heavyset man in his forties with a thick black mustache.

"The motel manager is certain it's the same man in the picture. He paid cash for the room yesterday. He hasn't seen him since."

The Oldsmobile with the stolen plates was parked right out front. There were only a few other cars in the parking lot.

"Shall we go find out?" Bosa suggested.

They all got out of the Suburban, hustled over to where two Mexican agents were huddled behind an old black Camaro. They held walkie-talkies. Mendoza shared a brief conversation in their native tongue and then turned to Eric and Bosa.

"He's inside the room. Our heat sensors have picked him up."

Eric stared at the decrepit one-story motel. Four doors down, he noticed two old Mexican men sitting in lawn chairs out front as if they had a makeshift porch in front of their motel room. Apparently, the Mexican agents had not informed them all hell could break loose, that they were about to confront and arrest one of the world's most dangerous assassins. The man would unlikely walk out with his hands in the air. The two men in the lawn chairs didn't look too worried, wearing their shorts and T-shirts, sipping on cervezas, the hot sun pouring down on them.

Mendoza gave his men more instructions. They spoke into their walkie-talkies. A half dozen more Mexican agents appeared from around the corner, and they all converged at the motel room door. Eric couldn't help but keep an eye on the two fat men in their lawn chairs, who monitored it all without expression, without talking, without much movement. He guessed the locals saw it all in Mexico.

Moments later, the Mexican agents burst through the door. Eric waited to hear gunfire, bombs, or some sort of escalating violence. But surprisingly, it all went down without incident. Which was the first red flag.

Mendoza listened to his radio, turned to Eric. "They got him."

"We shall see," Eric said, glancing at Bosa, unconvinced.

Eric nodded at the two Mexican men as he and Bosa followed Mendoza through the dirt parking lot. They did not return the nod, just sat there like bullfrogs. They barely moved except to lift their cheap beer to their lips. Eric entered the filthy motel room. A man was pinned to the tattered carpet by two of the Mexican agents, one putting cuffs on him. Eric knew immediately it was not the Caracal. He spotted drugs on a small table. A man of this caliber, a legend who gets paid tens of millions of dollars per hit, does not jeopardize his craft by getting high on cheap drugs in a dirty Mexican motel room.

"It's not him," Eric hissed to no one in particular.

One of the agents handed Mendoza a wallet. Flipping it open, Mendoza cursed in Spanish. At least, Eric figured it was cursing, because Mendoza repeated it several times before giving the wallet to him. Eric stared down at the picture on the driver's license. He had to admit the guy looked a lot like some of the photographs he'd seen of the Turk. But this man was named Bill Gleason of Maryland. There were matching credit cards and even pictures of his family. Eric found a business card.

Bill Gleason did not kill people for a living.

He sold carpet.

TWENTY-EIGHT

April gave up waiting on Trisha Sullivan to call her back after a long afternoon sitting at her office desk and staring at her burner phone. Everything in her gut said Trisha was a key player in all this. She had to find the woman, and knew where she lived. So she bolted from the office in the early evening without telling anyone. After playing the multiple-taxi-switch-up game again, she was dropped in Tarrytown, an affluent neighborhood with tree-canopied streets that hugged downtown. She stood in front of a white two-story Colonial with massive columns tucked away behind a black wrought iron security fence. The first time she'd been to the home was when Edward Sullivan and the other partners were recruiting the latest law school superstars. Eight of them had clerked with Michaels & Peterson the summer before her third year of law school. Sullivan threw a big crawfish boil in his backyard. He was originally from Louisiana and still had a slight Cajun drawl. It was a great party, with fabulous food and a live band. By the end of the summer, April had been one of two interns who had received a lucrative offer to join the firm. It had been 20 percent larger than her other offers. At the time, it had seemed like a dream come true. Now it felt like her worst nightmare.

She pushed through the walking gate on the front sidewalk and approached the estate. She spotted a red Honda Civic parked over to the left of the main driveway. She peered around the corner of the house toward the separate garage building. No sign of her boss's black Mercedes sedan or his fancy red Maserati. He was still at the office; she'd made sure of it earlier. April stepped up onto the front porch and knocked. She fidgeted while waiting, practicing what she'd say when Trisha opened the front door. The woman wasn't returning her phone calls, even though April clearly identified herself. Why? There was no way Trisha didn't recognize her name. Had something happened between the time she visited with Ben yesterday and now, that had spooked her?

The front door opened, but it wasn't Trisha. Instead, a Hispanic woman in her thirties answered, wearing a traditional black-and-white maid's outfit.

"Can I help you?" she asked.

"Hi, is Mrs. Sullivan home?"

"I'm sorry. She is not here at the moment."

April wondered if that were true. Could Trisha have asked her maid to turn away all visitors? The woman had been distraught when speaking with Ben.

"I'm a friend, not a stranger. She knows me."

April didn't necessarily want to identify herself. She didn't need the maid telling Edward Sullivan that she'd stopped by the house tonight.

"Mrs. Sullivan went to visit her sister this morning. She'll be out of town for the next week or so. I'm not exactly sure when she's returning."

April recalled Trisha mentioning a sister once during a conversation about their siblings. She'd been asking April all about her family and her two brothers. Her sister was a VP at a bank in Washington, DC. Because Trisha traveled so much to spend time with her sister, she and Edward had purchased a townhome there several years ago.

"Her sister in DC?" April asked, making sure she had it right.

"Yes. Would you like me to give her a message?"

"No, I'll reach out to her there. Thank you."

April walked away feeling even more frustrated. If Trisha Sullivan refused to call her back, the only way to speak with her was to go to DC.

TWENTY-NINE

Dean unexpectedly received a call back from Sally Kimble while he was walking through the Austin airport that evening after returning from Midland. He'd left her two voicemails earlier trying to gently coax her into giving them more information. She said she'd been praying a lot since seeing April yesterday. She felt it was time for her to be more forthright with what she knew. She was concerned about April's involvement. Dean just let her talk. He could tell she was getting there on her own. He didn't need to convince her of anything. She explained this was not easy for her. She wanted to help but feared for her kids. They were her life. She was in Austin proper to visit a cousin at a downtown hospital who'd just had a new baby. If he wanted to meet, she could slip away for a few minutes. They agreed on a pancake house near the hospital.

Dean parked his Jeep around the block from the restaurant behind a parking garage. He walked the sidewalks, hands in jacket pockets, eager to hear what Sally had to say—especially since his mind was still in spin mode from everything Hank Starch had shared with him up in Midland. He passed by a man out walking his golden retriever. A young couple strolled hand in hand, smiling and making lovebird eyes at each other. He thought of April. That had been them not long ago. Could it be them again? After this was all over? He had thought a lot about that while waiting in the airport all afternoon. More and more of these thoughts had been invading his brain. It'd been impossible for him to shut it down. Could she possibly feel the same way? He felt close to her again. But was it real? Or was it just because of the intense circumstances?

He circled the block from the parking garage, turned briskly around the corner, where he inadvertently bumped into another man who was headed the opposite way. They knocked shoulders. Dean spun around, apologized. But the other man just kept on walking without a word. He carried a black duffel bag in his hand and seemed to be in a hurry.

"Have a nice night," Dean muttered, continuing down the sidewalk.

He crossed the street, stepped through the parking lot outside of the pancake house, and headed inside. He found a booth near a front window. The restaurant was busy; people apparently enjoyed breakfast for dinner. A group of rowdy college kids made a lot of noise near the back. A few businessmen huddled in another corner. Several waitresses moseyed about, serving dishes, filling up coffee, calling people "dear" and "sweetie." Dean ordered a cup of caffeine, got comfortable in the booth, and watched the parking lot. He waited. Twenty minutes passed. She was late. He began to get a bad feeling. Maybe she'd had second thoughts. He couldn't blame her. In her shoes, he wasn't sure if he would show, either. She'd mentioned her kids three times in the first minute of their phone conversation.

He got two refills on the coffee, waited some more. He was about to give up when a dusty truck parked in a spot in the far corner of the well-lit parking lot. He watched a woman get out. Black jeans, tennis shoes, gray jacket. Her hair was straight, plain, not much style. She looked the appropriate age—late thirties. He knew it was her when he saw the eyes. They were unsteady, apprehensive. She stared at the pavement for a moment, seemed unsure whether she was going to walk toward the restaurant. She finally took hesitant steps toward the door.

Dean eased out of the booth to meet her at the front. He pushed through the glass door to greet her outside, wanting to immediately make her feel more comfortable. He didn't need her clamming up on him. They were within six feet of each other when it happened. Close enough for the blood to splatter across his shoes. One moment, Sally was stepping toward him; the next moment, she was collapsing to the pavement. Lifeless. The front part of her forehead missing, blood pooling everywhere. Screams began to fill the air as other people in the parking lot suddenly sobered up at the sight.

Dean frantically knelt to the ground over her.

Sally was dead. No doubt about it. No breathing. No movement. His stomach twisted violently. She'd been shot. But from where? And was another shot coming for him? Dean quickly stood, slid up next to the building to protect himself, and searched wildly across the street. His eyes absorbed the sidewalks, the parked cars, the trees, the buildings, and then up to the different levels of the parking garage. Someone had known about the meeting. Someone was tracking either Sally or him. And they'd just taken drastic measures to protect their secrets.

Two people who'd witnessed the shooting were simultaneously on their cell phones, screaming for 911. The rest of the crowd was fleeing at the sight. Dean felt panic seize him. He spun around, cut a path away from the madness. He made it to the edge of the parking lot, leaned over the hood of a car. He couldn't breathe. He felt like he would pass out. He turned to the pavement, his stomach swirling, and vomited by the tire. His head was spinning. He heard distant sirens swiftly approaching. He looked across the street again, stared up into the parking garage. His hands began to shake. The shooter had to be up there. A rifle, a scope, searching for him. He suddenly thought about April, too, and felt even more panic in his chest. Had someone already come for her? Pushing away from the bumper, he sprinted toward his car. He had to get to her.

THIRTY

The curtains in the hotel room were drawn tight. Dean stood near the window, rubbing his face in his hands. April sat on the bed, arms tucked around her knees, pale, still crying, and staring blankly at her bare feet. But she was safe. Dean had immediately called her on her burner after leaving the scene and told her to drop everything. He would pick her up ASAP. They went straight to the hotel, where he'd booked them a room. They both felt numb. What had happened to Sally was horrifying beyond words. Dean couldn't get his hands to stop shaking. He couldn't stop seeing her head explode just a few feet in front of him and watching the life instantly leave her body. They couldn't stop talking about her poor kids. All Sally cared about were her children. Taking care of them. Protecting them. And now they'd lost their mother in addition to their father a few years ago.

Dean knew he had to pull it together. Yes, this was awful. But he had to be smart or else he and April were next. He had to make sure someone paid for this. They were obviously getting close to the truth or Sally Kimble would not be dead right now.

They'd already filled each other in on the day's other crazy events, including her mission to track down Trisha Sullivan. They'd argued about April's next move. There was a big part of Dean that wanted her to get on a plane and just leave the country. But she refused. She would not allow Sally to die in vain. They went back and forth about it until he relented. If she left, they may not find Trisha. He wanted April to leave and stay at the same time. There was a tug-of-war going on inside him.

"We really should consider going to the feds," he suggested.

"What about the leak and what happened with that dead agent?"

"I know. I don't like it. But I trust my brother to protect you. We'll give Eric everything we know. Let him find Trisha Sullivan and take over from here."

Dean was hesitant about what he'd just said but didn't know where else to go from here. Everything had just exploded on them. It might be a risk. But going at it alone felt even riskier at this point.

"But Trisha might not talk to them. If we can find her, I think I can get her to talk to me. And if I go to the feds, then what do I do? Not only could someone clearly still get to me, they'd probably want me to testify somehow. Give my life up for the next couple of years to prosecute this crime—if they ever even get there with it. They'd probably put me in witness protection, change my name, my hair, my nose, and give me an exciting new career somewhere far away. I'd be Jane Smith from Ames, Iowa, and they'd have me stuffing mailboxes at the post office. What kind of life is that, Dean?"

He thought about what she said. She was being dramatic, of course, but there was a lot of truth in her words. "There has to be a better way."

"We go to DC," she insisted. "We see this through to the end."

"I can't put your life on the line, April."

"It's not your decision to make. It's mine."

He ran his hands through his hair and tugged on it. She was right. He couldn't force her to leave, and that was frustrating. "Okay, fine. We fly to DC first thing in the morning. Find her. And hopefully get the truth of what really happened."

"Good. It's settled."

He sat on the bed next to her. The weight of what had just happened hit him again. It just kept coming in waves. Sally Kimble was dead. And they'd personally walked her right up to the firing squad.

"How did they know, Dean?" April asked. Her voice was calmer now. Her eyes were red and puffy, but she'd gotten all the tears out. That well was empty.

"I don't know. They must've had her phone or mine. I'll get a new phone, just in case. But my guess is, they were still tracking her."

"So do you think they know all about me, too?"

"We have to proceed as if they do."

She processed that without much emotion. He could tell she was drained.

"What about her kids?" she asked again, shaking her head.

"I feel crushed about it, too. But we can't focus on them right now. We can't blame ourselves, and we can't get lost in our own grief. It won't bring Sally back. And it won't help us. I know that feels impossible right now, but we have to try."

"I know . . . I just . . . I can't believe it."

"It's late. You need to get some sleep, April. We both do. We're exhausted. We'll be able to think more clearly in the morning."

"You're probably right. Will you stay?"

"Of course. I can sleep in the chair in the corner."

THIRTY-ONE

Eric stood in the FBI war room staring at a digital wall filled with detailed information about their investigation. He'd slept for maybe three hours overnight and was back at the office well before sunrise. Unfortunately, none of what he saw before him had led to the capture of Yusuf Demir. The trail for the Caracal had grown ice-cold. The pressure was building. Everyone in the world wanted to know who'd pulled the trigger that killed Senator Carson. The media had quickly turned on them. Politicians were already playing the blame game. The current narrative was that the FBI was failing. Eric couldn't argue with that, considering one of their own had betrayed them. The director didn't want this information shared with the public yet. Not when it would certainly compromise their investigation. The director wanted to make a breakthrough on the case first. Then they could lead with the positive before opening themselves up to the negative.

Up till this point, Eric had chosen to protect their inside information about Demir, believing they'd find more success tracking him in secret without a huge spotlight shining directly on their pursuit. But things had gotten more desperate. So he'd decided to change tactics. They were now going to use the media and the public in their hunt for the Caracal. Maybe they would catch a break if they plastered his many faces all over the TV and internet. It was bound to leak soon anyway.

Might as well be proactive with it and gain some positive media coverage. However, he knew once they did, they had a limited window of opportunity to get him before he disappeared.

His team had created a digital media kit that was set to be emailed to all major news outlets upon his final approval this morning. The kit included photographs of Demir, a brief biography, and a list of suspected assassinations around the world. It was standard press material. They would include a website and a toll-free number for people to reach out with any information. The director had also approved significant financial rewards for information that led to his capture and arrest. Eric knew it would be a logistical nightmare. A team of eight agents was already set up in a room in DC with phones and computers, just to handle the barrage of phone calls and emails. There would likely be thousands from all over the world. His team would have to sift through the nonsensical crap and pursue those that seemed legitimate.

Agent Brewster entered the war room. "You see this, boss?"

Brewster handed him a digital tablet. On the screen was a local Austin story about the shooting death of a woman at a downtown restaurant last night. Sally Kimble. Thirty-nine. Single gunshot wound to the back of the head. Suspect still at large.

"I recognize that name," Eric said.

"Really? From where?"

"She used to work for my father. What happened here?"

"I just spoke with the detective in charge. He said it was a mess. Said he has a buddy who was a marine sniper back in the day. Guy used to share kill photos with him. The detective in charge of this said this scene reminded him of that. A distant but perfect shot to the junction of the brain and brain stem. In his words, *a professional kill.* The woman's head was obliterated. A lot of people saw it. They said one second she was walking through the parking lot; the next, she's dead. But no one ever saw a shooter. But this is why I'm bringing it to your attention. Detective said they recovered the bullet. A .338 Lapua Magnum."

Eric cursed. "Are you serious?"

"Yes, sir."

Eric ran a hand over his bald head. The .338 Lapua Magnum was the same ammunition used to assassinate Senator Carson two nights ago.

"Find out everything you can about Sally Kimble."

THIRTY-TWO

Dean stood at his editor's office window early the next morning.

April was still at the hotel. They had booked separate flights, just to be safe. If they were somehow tracking him, Dean didn't want it to lead to her. She would leave first. He would join her in DC. She seemed to be doing better after some sleep. Steadier. Less fragile. He was battling a severe ache in his neck and back. Sleeping in that uncomfortable hotel chair had done him no favors.

"What time is she leaving?" Harvey asked.

"An hour before me."

"How long will you be gone?"

"Not long, if all goes well. But then nothing has gone as planned."

Dean grabbed the current edition of the *Austin American-Statesman* newspaper from Harvey's desk, again scanned the article that summarized the bizarre murder of thirty-nine-year-old Sally Kimble last night in the parking lot of a pancake house downtown. Police had no current suspects. They were searching for a person of interest who'd fled the scene. Dean knew that *he* was that person. The investigation was ongoing. There were a few dramatic quotes from witnesses and the standard police promise to pursue the killer at all costs. Dean had already spoken with the beat reporter this morning, without letting him know of his involvement. The reporter didn't know much else. The police were baffled. Looked like a professional kill. They were devouring the area for clues. Lots of eyewitnesses, but no one saw a shooter.

"You mentioned a potential breakthrough on the phone," Dean said, getting around to official business.

"You remember the mention of 'Scorpion' in the initial text exchange between Edward Sullivan and Lamar Rainer? *Scorpion green-lights.*"

"Yes."

"I think I've identified the Scorpion."

"Are you serious?"

"Don't look so shocked. This ain't my first rodeo, you know. I was already doing your job when you were still in diapers, son."

"I know, boss. You remind me of that at least three times a week. Who is it?"

"Ever heard the name Hossle Jester?"

"No."

"Oilman. Grew up in Port Lavaca, a small town of twelve thousand near the coast. Real hell-raiser as a youth. Spent years in juvenile detention because of all the fights he got into at school over the years. When he was fifteen, he nearly killed a boy who tried to steal his girlfriend by placing a giant scorpion in the kid's gym shorts. Kid got stung and spent two weeks in the ICU before finally recovering. I guess folks around town started calling Jester the Scorpion after that. After he dropped out of high school, Jester's uncle gave him a job as a roughneck on one of his oil rigs. He got his first taste in the oil business. His uncle was a ruthless businessman who bullied, extorted, and bribed to get what he wanted. Jester learns the business that way. His uncle gets stabbed to death in an alley behind a bar one night when Jester is in his mid-twenties. Perpetrator is never caught. Most believe Hossle Jester killed his uncle himself to take over his business. By the time Jester is thirty, he's grown a small company to one worth over ten million dollars. He's now worth hundreds of millions."

Harvey handed Dean a digital tablet. On the screen was an image of a sixtysomething man in a black suit. His hair was gray. His face hard.

"Jester remains a troublemaker," Harvey continued. "He just has more power and influence. For the next thirty years, Jester steals, bribes, and bullies his way to explosive growth. As he's gotten wealthier, he's apparently also gotten crazier and more private. Stays mostly out of the spotlight. He now has dozens of companies that operate under different shell corporations, according to my business sources. He started pouring tens of millions into politics decades ago, local and national, playing both sides, looking for favor and governmental protection. They claim he owns half the Texas legislature, and that he's the real reason the governor got elected six years ago. Jester has his own private island here on Lake Travis. The island is like Fort Knox. He apparently built a fifteen-foot stone wall around it and has armed guards and attack dogs. You can't get near it. The man is crazy. A private helicopter takes him back and forth to the governor's mansion, where he has designs to put him in the White House one day soon."

Dean studied the photograph. "I think I remember the name 'Hossle Jester.' Was one of his companies involved in the big offshore oil spill two years ago?"

Harvey sipped his coffee, nodded. "That's correct. Killed seventeen people and created one of the biggest oil-spill debacles the gulf has ever seen. A real mess. They made him and a half dozen other high-ranking executives from other oil companies testify in front of Senate and congressional hearings on Capitol Hill last year. It's still ongoing. Could end up costing these companies tens of billions of dollars, depending on how the blame gets shifted around. A lot of finger-pointing. A lot of name-calling. A lot of jockeying for position in DC. Some of these companies could collapse if it goes the wrong way."

"What makes you think that he's the Scorpion referenced in our situation?"

"Eastwood Petroleum."

Dean registered the name. The oil company that basically gave away a block of gulf land to J. Walter Petroleum in Lease Sale 151. "Eastwood is one of his companies?"

"Yes, according to one of my sources. Although you'd have to dig to find it."

Dean looked at the angry face of the old man in the picture. "So you think Jester paid someone to have Carson assassinated?"

Harvey shrugged. "I think he's crazy enough to do it."

"But why?"

"Not sure yet. It's your job to find that out."

"I'm trying, boss. I really am."

Harvey said, "Fred is getting nervous."

Fred Morley was the owner and publisher of *TexasNow*.

"He's always nervous."

"Neither of us wants a dead source. Or a dead reporter."

"But he still wants the story."

"Of course."

"So then no one is asking me to back off, right?"

"We just want you to be extra careful. Don't be stupid. This story is not worth your own safety."

"Tell Fred not to worry about me."

Truthfully, Dean *was* nervous. Being so close to a killer's bullet had made it difficult to sleep last night and then step back out onto an open sidewalk this morning. His eyes were searching for a shooter in every possible direction.

"He's not, believe me. But he doesn't want to lose this thing. He's pushing me to publish what we've got right now, just in case."

"In case I get killed?"

"It's a big story already, Dean. A home run. Even without knowing the full conclusion."

"We can't publish something now. We put this out now, we give the bad guys a chance to run for the hills. They may get away with it. We can't let that happen."

"I know that. I've been able to settle Fred down. So far, I've convinced him to forgo a home run when we could be getting close to hitting a grand slam in the bottom of the ninth in the World Series. Fred liked that language. But he wants you to check in multiple times a day with a full report until this is done."

Dean nodded, walked back to the window. He rubbed his stiff neck. Stupid chair. He thought about April. It was hard to leave the hotel room this morning, not knowing what the day would bring. Not knowing if he was certain to see her again. They were living moment to moment, and it scared them both. Once more he thought of calling Eric, telling him everything, and begging him to protect April. But he knew April would never forgive him for that. And if something happened to her while under FBI protection, he would never be able to forgive himself.

"How are you doing?" Harvey asked.

"I'm okay."

"I'm serious, son. This has been a crazy couple of days."

Dean sighed, let his guard down. "I don't know, boss. I'm trying. I'm exhausted. I haven't slept well. Now I have the blood of an innocent woman with four children on my hands. Hard to process all of that. I can't, really. On top of all that, I'm trying very hard not to fall in love again with a woman who's counting on me to help her live through all this mess. At the moment, she's a source. Nothing more. I need to treat her like that. But it feels impossible. I'm way too close to all of this."

Harvey put a hand on his shoulder. "Did I ever tell you my city council story?"

Dean shook his head, wondered if this was the time for more of Harvey's stories.

"So it's 1986, and I'm working at *The Boston Globe*, investigating the story of a city councilman who's been accused of skimming money from city accounts. Somebody passes a number along to me, says I should contact this source. So I do. A woman. I don't even know her name. Just have her phone number. I tell this woman who I am and some details of the story I'm working. Over the course of the next two months, she secretly feeds me critical internal documents that not only undermine the councilman's constant denial of any wrongdoing but also exposes a whole web of city government corruption. It was a major story and my first big break. Made headlines everywhere. For the entire two months, I never met my source. We communicated through a complex system of phone calls, newspaper switches, and random drop-offs, real Watergate conspiracy stuff. No emails and text messages in those days."

Dean looked over at him. "So you never met her?"

"Yes, eventually. After it was all over. And then I married her."

Dean smiled, surprised. "Janice? Seriously?"

Harvey nodded. "She worked on the inside. A woman of strong conviction and morality, much like your April. When she became aware of the corruption, she was determined to hold those in charge accountable and help change the system."

"I never knew that."

Harvey shrugged. "Maybe you'll be sharing a similar story years from now."

A staff assistant poked her head in the door. "Something is up, Mr. Kingsley. Turn on the TV."

Harvey flipped on his office TV. A breaking-news alert suddenly hit the screen. The news anchor began talking about information just released by the FBI related to the assassination of Senator Carson. The FBI had identified a main suspect: Yusuf Demir, a Turkish assassin also known as the Caracal, who was wanted around the globe. There were over a dozen prominent kills attached to his name, although no one was certain how many were legitimate and how many were myth. The anchor went on to read some of these famous kills. The FBI believed he pulled the trigger in Carson's death from a perch outside of Carson's security detail. They also believed he could still be in the United States. He was a very dangerous man. Four pictures of Demir popped up on the screen. He looked different in each picture. Some with dark hair, some with light, some with facial hair, some without. A website and phone number were listed below them. The FBI was offering a financial reward for any information that led to his capture and arrest.

Dean's eyes settled on the picture of Demir in the bottom-right corner. It was a straightforward image of just the assassin's face. Gray hair and dark-gray beard. Rugged and angry. Dean studied the face. His mind began to process, a reel slowly playing. Why did he know that face? Those eyes? And why was it so fresh in his brain? Then it hit him like a punch to the gut. He loudly cursed.

"What?" Harvey glanced over to him.

"I've seen him, Harvey."

"Who?"

"Yusuf Demir." Dean cursed softly again. "Last night! I saw this guy just last night."

"Where?"

"I can't believe this. I bumped into him on my way to meet Sally Kimble last night. I was turning the corner; we bumped shoulders. I apologized. He was a real jerk. Just kept on walking. He was carrying a big bag. He was right there in front of me."

"Are you sure?"

Dean found a guest chair, sat, feeling nauseous again. "Positive. He probably had his rifle in the bag with him. I swear it was him. The man who killed Carson was the same guy who shot Sally Kimble."

Harvey stared back at the television. "Maybe we should go to the feds."

Dean had not yet told Harvey about the FBI leak that led to the death of Carson. He wanted to protect his brother. That conversation was off the record. And he valued family above everything.

Dean looked up. "We can't."

"Why? I don't like taking all these risks. If what you say is true, I'm lucky to not be planning your funeral right now."

"Just give me twenty-four hours."

THIRTY-THREE

April took a cab to a Target. But she first made the curious cab driver zig and zag through three different neighborhoods. He kept staring in his rearview mirror at her like she was crazy, but she didn't care. She said she wanted to look at some real estate. If they had somehow followed her to the hotel, waited all night, and then they were still back there this morning, she would admit defeat and personally pay for their airline tickets. They could sit right beside her. Oscar on her right, Felix on her left. They could finally get to know each other a little better. Enough of these games.

She thought about Dean. It was difficult to watch him walk out of the hotel room this morning. She felt safer with him. Her feelings for him were gradually being reignited, and she wasn't sure what to do with those feelings. She had no idea where all this was leading. Their entire future was up in the air.

Inside Target, she quickly purchased blue jeans, shirts, jackets, sweaters, underwear, tennis shoes, some toiletries, and a travel bag. It was enough to hold her for a few days. She had no idea how long she would be gone. She changed clothes in the restroom, then called for another cab.

She eyed the parking lot through the glass doors. For a fleeting moment, she thought she spotted the thick guy, Felix, getting out of a car. Her heart pounded beneath the jacket. But then he opened the back door and a kid bounced out. She breathed easy again, but she wondered how much longer she could put herself through this roller coaster. She tugged her new Dallas Cowboys cap low on her forehead, her brown hair tucked beneath, and pushed through the glass doors to the parking lot. She slid into the back seat of the cab, eased down into the battered vinyl.

"The airport," she said, and the cab whisked her away.

THIRTY-FOUR

His flight left thirty minutes late.

Dean thought of sleeping. He was exhausted, but he knew he would not sleep soundly again until this whole thing was over. April had gotten on the plane safe and sound. Her text had relayed that reassuring message. This helped him relax just a bit. They'd both gotten out of the city, away from the bloody carnage of the previous night, and hopefully they were about to get some real answers.

While in the air, Dean connected to the in-flight Wi-Fi and began searching for video clips of Hossle Jester testifying about the oil spill disaster in front of Senate and congressional hearings last year. Jester sat in a blue suit that looked one size too big for his older, frail body. His hair was gray and thinning on top. His face was wrinkled and looked beaten from years under direct sunlight while out on oil rigs. The eyes were tiny and dark. He looked angry at having to sit there and answer questions from stupid politicians. Many of whom he'd probably helped put into office. Some of them took it easy on him. Others went after him harder. Jester's temper flared throughout. It was clear he wasn't used to having to answer to anyone. And he didn't like it one bit. He kept snapping back at certain committee members. Dean noticed Jester's team of lawyers sitting behind him shifting uncomfortably throughout the session. They'd likely encouraged their client to stay calm and collected, but it was clear he was defying those instructions. After watching clips for nearly an hour, Dean believed this was the kind of man who would have someone killed. There didn't appear to be much compassion inside of him. But would he really pay an international assassin to eliminate a future president?

The plane made a noon descent into Reagan National. From his window seat, Dean watched the sun begin to dip. He also noticed a city now gripped in the clutches of bitter cold. Snow had been pushed around the airstrips. A surprising winter storm front had moved through. The earliest DC had experienced in three decades, according to news reports. He wasn't in Texas anymore.

He zipped up his leather jacket, struggled down the aisle with the other travelers. Stepping off the plane into the connecting walkway, he immediately felt the chill through the cracks. Someone ahead of him said it was currently twenty-two degrees, with the wind chill taking it even lower. Dean shook his head, adjusted his bag on his shoulder. He navigated the busy airport, found an outside curb. A gust of frigid air nearly knocked him over. Tiny puffs of visible breath leaked out of mouths all around him. The wisest of souls were bundled up tight. Dean flagged down a taxi. A young man who introduced himself as Ricky took his bag, dropped it into the trunk. He wore a puffy Commanders jacket and thick leather gloves. They both climbed inside the vehicle.

Twisting around, Ricky asked, "Where to, man?"

"Park Hyatt."

"Nice."

Ricky placed his gloved hands on the steering wheel, flung the taxi into heavy traffic. Cars honked all around them. It didn't seem to faze Ricky, who tuned the radio to a gospel station and began to sing along.

He looked at Dean in the mirror. "Here on business?"

"Yep." Dean wasn't in the mood for small talk. "How cold is it gonna get tonight?"

"Probably in the teens, maybe some more snow. Where you coming from?"

"Sixty degrees and clear skies."

Ricky laughed. "Welcome to DC."

It was a short trip to the hotel. Ricky decided he would carry the conversation, so he rambled on about different sports. Said he was a lifelong NFL fan and had played a little tailback at a small college in Michigan. Could've made it to the pros if he hadn't busted up his knee. Dean ignored most of it and studied the city through a foggy, smudged window.

Ricky finally pulled them up to the Park Hyatt hotel.

Dean tipped him well, grabbed his small bag, and entered the hotel lobby. April had chosen the hotel. It was very nice. Too nice for a reporter making peanuts, but Harvey was letting him put everything on the website's credit card. His editor had used the words "Be conservative" about six times before handing it over.

Dean collected his room key and took the elevator to the seventh floor. He was eager to find April on the other side of the door. Being away from her for even a few hours had caused him serious anxiety. He didn't want to do it again. Not until this was all over.

THIRTY-FIVE

Eric still couldn't believe his father's former secretary was the woman who'd been killed by a professional hit last night. Although Eric had never met Sally Kimble in person, he recalled speaking with her a couple of times over the years when she was making calls on behalf of his father. A small, cruel world. According to quick research by his team, she'd apparently left the law firm four months ago, right after his father had passed away, and had spent the past few months doing part-time bookkeeping work for an accounting firm out in Marble Falls. The thin file they'd put together showed her widowed with four kids. There wasn't anything more interesting. So why the hell had a shooter just taken her out?

Eric stood in the same parking lot where Sally had been shot dead last night. At his request, Austin PD still had the whole thing blocked off with yellow tape. Eric's own FBI crime scene unit was scouring the area for clues, including searching area buildings and parking garages for the exact shooter location. So far, nothing. He wiped his wet head with his hand. Gray afternoon clouds had rolled in, and it was starting to sprinkle.

Agent Brewster stood beside him going over every detail the APD detective had shared with him so far. "They tracked down Sally Kimble's cousin—a woman named Nicole Amber—who just gave birth to a new baby girl over at Dell Seton. She says Sally came into Austin proper to see her and the new baby last night, and then she said she had to leave to meet someone here at this restaurant. Sally told her she'd be back shortly. Nicole wasn't sure whom she was meeting. But she said Sally seemed preoccupied the entire time they were visiting together. Something was bothering her."

"The restaurant have security cameras?" Eric asked.

"Yeah. But the place was half full. And she never made it inside."

"I still want to see the footage."

"I have it. APD found nothing of interest inside her vehicle. Just a small purse with the usual contents. We just pulled up the call logs from her cell phone."

"Let me see them."

Brewster handed over a digital tablet. Eric stared at the screen. Kimble had called out and/or received ten phone calls yesterday. Most of them had names attached from her own phone's contacts. Nicole Amber was listed four different times on the log. Eric squinted at a number without contact information that appeared three times yesterday. Why did it look familiar? This person had called Sally Kimble at 7:32 yesterday morning. Again at 11:14 a.m. Then Sally had called the same number back at 7:17 p.m. last night. Just thirty minutes before she'd been killed a few feet away.

Something made Eric pull out his own phone, type in the same phone number. He cursed out loud. Dean Dawson. His brother. He couldn't believe it. Eric now felt sure this had something to do with the Carson assassination. It was too big a coincidence. His brother was on the story and knew far more than he was willing to share the other night. That pissed Eric off. A woman had been killed. If Dean had told him what he was chasing down, Eric might have been able to prevent the death.

"Can you pull up the security footage for me?" he asked Brewster.

Brewster took the digital tablet back, punched a few times on the screen, and then handed it back to him. "Camera one is inside. Camera two is parking lot."

Eric pressed on camera one. He studied the faces of those people inside the restaurant just before Sally Kimble arrived. He pinched the screen with his fingers to tighten the focus on several of them. And then he cursed again. Dean was sitting in a booth by himself watching the parking lot through a front window. Two minutes before Sally's demise, Eric watched as his younger brother got up from the booth, walked over to the front door, stepped outside, and stood there as Sally approached. After she collapsed to the pavement, Dean darted through the growing crowd. His brother was the person of interest the police had mentioned had fled the scene. Why did he run? What was going on? Eric was suddenly hit with another emotion. Fear. His brother could've also been killed. Was he even safe at the moment?

Eric immediately called Dean. No answer. So he left an urgent message.

"Bro, call me back! Right now! I mean it!"

THIRTY-SIX

April cracked the door, cautiously peeked out.

"It's me," Dean said.

The door shut, the chains rattled, and then she pulled it open.

She wore a thin beige sweater and blue jeans. Bare feet. She looked tired. Her eyes were red, but so were his. The result of tears and fatigue. She let him inside and locked the door behind him. It was a standard hotel room with two beds, a small table, a dresser, and a television. It had a good view of the city.

Dean set his bag down, walked to the window, admired the nation's capital.

"Did you get here okay?" he asked.

"Yes, I think so. It's been a long day already."

"I presume Trisha still hasn't called you back?"

She shook her head. "I've tried several more times. She's not biting. She might not even be using that phone anymore. Probably a burner phone like mine. Her normal cell phone is on file at the firm, and it's not the same number. But I was able to get her DC address. Georgetown."

She sat on the bed, tucked her feet beneath her. The television was on with the sound muted. Cable news. The first thing Dean saw on the screen was the face of the assassin, a face that had haunted him the entire flight. He was undecided on telling April about his encounter with Yusuf Demir last night. She was already on pins and needles. He didn't want to freak her out even more. He tried not to think too much about it himself. He checked his phone again. Eric had been repeatedly calling and even left him four text messages. What did he want? Dean had no intention of calling him back. There was no conversation he could have with his brother right now with everything that had unfolded over the past eighteen hours. He felt bad about it but had no choice.

He peered out the window again. "It's cold here, April."

"Wimp."

"Hey, cut me some slack. I'm a Texas boy. My toes freeze easily."

"I like it. Reminds me of law school. The winter months were always fun in Virginia. It's been hard to dream of a white Christmas in Texas."

"I'm perfectly okay with that."

She grinned. Then she joined him at the window.

"Tell me everything Harvey said this morning," she said.

Dean had texted her earlier saying he had big updates to share when he arrived. So he spent the next ten minutes pacing the room and filling her in on everything his editor had discovered about the wealthy oilman, Hossle Jester.

"No wonder I couldn't find him," April said. "'Scorpion' is a nickname. Not a company or a project."

"Exactly."

"Harvey is nervous?"

"Yes, and so is my publisher. Fred wants to go public now with what information we have before this somehow slips away from us. I'm on a short leash."

"What do you want to do?"

Dean wanted to say a few things. *Walk over and kiss you right now. Beg your forgiveness. Run away together.* But she was only talking about his story.

"Keep you safe," he said. "I'm just not sure the best way to do that right now."

"I feel safe with you here. You hungry?"

"Starving."

"Room service?"

"Yes, please. Then let's go find Trisha Sullivan."

THIRTY-SEVEN

Eric called Dean for the fourth time today and then nearly threw his phone against the wall when it again went to his voicemail. His brother was either intentionally ignoring him, or he was dead. Because Eric refused to consider the latter, he let himself believe Dean was simply chasing this story. He had a lead that had somehow put him one step ahead of the FBI. There was no other explanation as to why he was meeting with Sally Kimble when Eric barely knew she even existed. So what was that lead? Eric and his team could find no connection between Sally and the assassination of Senator Carson. It felt like a million miles between those two points. But there had to be something there if Yusuf Demir was the man who'd pulled the trigger that killed both. He also couldn't shake something else. Was it a coincidence this woman happened to be his father's legal secretary for more than a decade? He didn't normally believe in coincidences. So how was all this tied together? What could Dean possibly know? He also couldn't stop thinking about his conversation with his brother the other night. Dean had brought up his father. He said he'd been thinking a lot about him lately. Another coincidence? Unlikely.

Eric had originally wanted to handle this brother-to-brother without involving the full force of the FBI. But because that wasn't working, he finally sent agents over to Dean's workplace and to his apartment.

Reports just came back that his brother was not at either location. His editor had the audacity to claim he'd gone on vacation. He thought a beach somewhere but wasn't sure. Dean's editor was clearly messing with his agents, lying, covering. Eric told his guys to stick around until they found him. Monitor his apartment. Surveil his workplace. He even gave instructions to follow his editor.

Eric sent one last text to his brother.

You're really pissing me off.

He then walked into a room where a video conference had been set up with Special Agent Thomas Elliott out of DC. Elliott had requested the meeting. He said they had something interesting he wanted to share with him. Agent Brewster was also in the room with him. A tech connected the call. Moments later, Eric was staring at Elliott, a forty-something guy with bright-red hair, a mustache, and caterpillars for eyebrows, who was sitting at a table looking right back at him. They had worked closely together on several cases when Eric was in DC.

"Hey, man," Elliott said. "How're you doing?"

"Been better."

"I bet. Well, I may have something to brighten your mood."

"Tell me."

"We've got a local prostitute here who says she may know something about the assassination and wants the reward money we offered up today."

"A prostitute? You can't be serious, Thomas."

"Bear with me, bud. I promise I would not set up this call without checking into this first. Turns out this gal is one of our city's classier hookers. Works for one of the high-dollar executive outfits that cater to DC's rich and famous. She probably makes more than you and me combined. She claims she was paid five times her normal amount earlier this year to seduce someone who turned out to be important in political circles."

Eric sighed. Not surprising. Another politician cheating on his spouse.

"Who?" he asked.

"Senator Ted Lambert."

"Florida?"

"Yep. She identified him through online images. We checked into it and confirmed through security footage that Lambert was indeed at the St. Regis hotel on the night of her accusation. Same footage showed her there. She says she was paid in cash to do this by a man who never identified himself. She was instructed to get Lambert back to her hotel suite. And make sure they did it on the bed with the lights on. This gal is certain someone recorded it. She recalls the same man who hired her coming into their hotel room in the middle of the night, with Lambert still passed out on the bed next to her and fiddling with some box on the dresser. Then he quietly left. She pretended to be asleep the entire time, but she saw the whole thing."

"She ever see or speak to this guy again?"

"No. But this is where it gets interesting. She says she was watching the news a few months after and recognized the man who hired her on TV. Mark Edmonds, chief of staff for Senator Carson."

"She's sure of it?"

"She swears by it."

"You got any footage of him on the hotel property?"

"Not yet. We're digging. And still talking with her."

"Let me know if you find out anything else."

Ending the video call, Eric gave a quick thought to Senator Lambert. Late forties, married, with what he thought were two teenage daughters. Been in the DC political game for probably fifteen years. Rising star. A quick presidential campaign this past year before Senator Carson ran away with it.

"You think Carson blackmailed Lambert?" Brewster asked.

"Possibly. Carson played dirty with everyone. People feared him because of it."

"Feels like a huge stretch to believe Lambert would retaliate by hiring an assassin."

"Definitely. Unless something much bigger was at play here. Plus, Lambert's not super wealthy. I think he owned a construction company before jumping into politics. No family money. Yusuf Demir has been known to charge up to twenty-five million per job."

"Someone else could have footed the bill for him."

"True. I want to speak with Senator Lambert myself. Find him."

THIRTY-EIGHT

Dean and April took a cab from the hotel in the early afternoon.

The address was listed in Georgetown, a posh area not far from the hotel. The cab driver pulled to a curb and pointed to a strand of picturesque row houses, all slender and colorful. The Sullivans owned a three-level cream Victorian situated in the middle. April showed him photos of the home on Trisha's Instagram account. They were at the right place. They paid the driver and got out. Soft flakes of snow were falling from the sky. April tightened her puffy black coat, which she said she'd purchased at Target, and wrapped a red scarf around her neck. Dean felt the chill from head to toe. He'd underdressed and underpacked. He wished for long underwear and a hunting jacket. April was right. He was a wimp. Dean moved up the steps to the front door. No lights were on in the windows. The house looked dark on all levels. He peered in a window by the door. No movement. He couldn't see much at all.

"I don't think anybody is home," he said.

She knocked on the door. They waited a few seconds. Dean rocked on his heels, stared up and down the street. An old man was out walking his two golden retrievers. Dean gave him a cordial nod. It was a quiet neighborhood street without much traffic. A couple of cars parked on curbs here and there. His eyes did a quick scan and then returned to the door.

"Try the buzzer," Dean suggested.

She punched the small button. Still no answer. Dean put his hand on the doorknob, turned. It was unlocked, surprising them both. They exchanged a concerned glance. He pushed the door more fully open. The entry foyer was dark.

"Hello?" Dean called into the home. Nothing.

He turned to April. "What do you think?"

She pushed past him and entered the dark house.

"Hello?" April tried again, louder. There was still no response.

April gasped. "Dean!"

He moved in beside her. A narrow wooden desk in the hallway was overturned, the drawers yanked out onto the hardwood floor. Papers were spread across the hallway. Dean instinctively pushed April behind him, looked for a weapon of some sort. He found an umbrella hanging from a coatrack, grabbed it, gripping it like a baseball bat. He still had a powerful swing. His muscles tightened. The stairs were straight ahead. He stepped forward, ready to pounce on anything that moved. He stuck his head into the living room, found another light switch. April gripped his arm. This room was also ransacked. The coffee table was flipped upside down. The sofa cushions tossed about, books and pictures scattered everywhere. A disaster zone.

"They were here," April whispered.

"But are they still here?"

They carefully navigated through the mess, moving into a dining area, where all the chairs were overturned. Some were splintered to pieces. He flipped on lights as they moved through the rooms, still gripping the umbrella, just in case he had to swing for the fences. The kitchen was destroyed as well, but there were still no signs of life. Or death. Which was what Dean feared the most. He found a picture frame on the floor, stared at Edward and Trisha Sullivan in formal wear. He set the frame on the counter. They returned to the stairs.

"I'm going up," Dean said. "You stay here."

"Not a chance."

Dean frowned. "Please, April."

"I'm going with you," she said, brow pinched.

"Fine. So much for chivalry."

They took careful and quiet steps up the staircase. On the second level, Dean peered around the corner, found different items flung about on the carpet in the hallway. Clothes, boxes, books. He felt for a knob and the hallway glowed. There were two doors on each side. They discovered bedrooms completely torn apart, a study in shambles. The whole house had been destroyed. Whoever had been here had searched every corner, ripped out every hidden compartment, in search of something. They found the master bedroom at the end of the hallway. It was ripped apart as well. Dean paused in the doorway, hearing something from the bathroom. The door was partially cracked. The light was on inside. Running water. He felt sweat form on his palms.

He turned to April, begged her in a whisper, "Please stay here."

This time she conceded without a fight.

Dean stepped over a box, approached the bathroom. His heart pounded in his ears. He took a deep breath, counted silently to three, pushed the door open. The bathroom was empty. He exhaled. Someone had left the faucet running in the sink. He turned it off, returned to April.

"Let's check upstairs," he said. "And then get out of here."

They raced up the staircase to the third level, where they walked into one large room that had been converted into an art studio. He turned on a light, and they quickly searched the corners. There was no sign of Trisha Sullivan lying dead somewhere, and for this they were at least relieved. Dean paused by a window, looked down into the street below. His eyes narrowed. He noticed a plain gray Buick parked across the way that had not been sitting there when they arrived. And then a knot formed in his throat. There was a man sitting behind the wheel. Mid-thirties, short hair, clean-shaven. He wasn't on the phone. He wasn't doing anything. Just waiting. And his eyes were locked on the front door of the Sullivans' row house. Who was he? Had he seen them enter the house? Was he waiting for them to leave to follow them?

"Time to go, April."

"Do you think she's dead?"

"I don't think so. I think we would've found her."

"I hope you're right."

They hurried back downstairs. April began turning off the lights, wanting to leave the house like they found it, but Dean stopped her.

"Why?"

"Gut feeling. Let's go out the back."

They stepped outside the back door. Then they followed a narrow driveway behind all the row houses before returning to the front sidewalk again farther down the same street. Dean took a glance back up the street. The man was out of the car and approaching the row house. Was he going inside to find them?

"What's going on?" April asked him.

"Someone is watching the house. He saw us inside."

Dean pointed up the street.

April's eyes narrowed. "You think he followed us here?"

"I don't know. Could be the same guy who trashed the place before we ever arrived."

"That doesn't make me feel any better."

The guy suddenly peered down the sidewalk right at them. They'd been spotted.

"Let's go!" he said, grabbing April's arm.

They walked swiftly down the sidewalk, away from the guy. As they passed a thick tree, Dean took his first peek over his shoulder. He cursed to himself. The man was following and trailing in the shadows. Dean surveyed the street ahead, developing a plan in his mind. They were approaching an intersection. An old stone mansion sat on the corner, surrounded by a short wrought iron fence lined with thick bushes.

"He's still back there," Dean mentioned.

"What do we do?"

"Follow my lead."

They turned the street corner at the intersection. When they were just out of view, Dean moved rapidly. He found a gap in the bushes, helped lift April up and over the wrought iron fence. She landed on the other side and kept her balance on the frozen grass. Dean then wrapped his hands around the sharp points of the fence and hoisted himself up. He swung his legs over and also landed in the grass. He then guided them both behind the thick bushes and hid. Seconds later, Dean spotted the guy pass by them on the sidewalk. The man's head swiveled both ways, searching the sidewalks. He stepped forward and then stopped. He was looking in all directions. He then took off in a hurry up the sidewalk, realizing he'd lost the two of them.

In the clear, Dean and April crossed through the front yard of the mansion, found another small gap in the bushes on the opposite street, climbed over the fence, and returned to the other sidewalk. Then they raced back toward where they'd come. Dean found an alleyway between building clusters. They tucked themselves behind a smelly dumpster. They were safe. For now.

"We should switch hotels, just in case," he suggested.

"You think?"

"Better to be safe. Somewhere smaller, more obscure. Where we can pay cash."

"Okay."

"Any idea how we find Trisha Sullivan now?"

"Her sister. She's a bank executive somewhere in the city. I need to do some research to figure out where and go talk with her."

"Okay, we'll split up for now," Dean suggested, putting a plan together. "If this guy was watching us, they'll still be looking for us together. I'll go back to the hotel, get our bags, and then meet up with you. You go find the sister."

THIRTY-NINE

Eric took the FBI jet to DC and arrived in the late afternoon. He was then whisked away by a local agent and dropped in front of the Russell Senate Office Building, which sat a block from the US Capitol Building. Senator Ted Lambert's office suite was on the second floor. Eric had called earlier to confirm Lambert was still at the office and available to see him. Eric hadn't been paying much attention to the political climate surrounding the assassination and what it meant for the upcoming election. A member of his team had updated him on the plane. Behind the scenes, Lambert had been trying to whip up support to be a last-minute replacement for Carson on the presidential ticket. Most believed he had a legitimate shot to beat out Senator Carson earlier this year for the party nomination. Which was why it was a surprise to everyone when he unexpectedly pulled out of the race and threw his support behind his adversary. Eric now knew why.

Eric arrived by himself, to appear as unassuming and friendly as possible. He didn't want the senator to immediately be on the defensive. A female aide led him through the office suite and over to a corner office. Senator Lambert sat behind a desk, the desk lamp on, his suit jacket hanging on a coatrack by the door. At forty-eight, Lambert had a nice head of dark hair with only touches of gray throughout. He could pass for late thirties. He was in excellent shape, had a charismatic personality, and most people from both sides liked him, even if they disagreed on particular issues. He'd first been elected to the Senate nine years ago after spending the first six of his career as a congressman.

Lambert stood and greeted Eric near the door.

"Thank you for stopping by, Agent Dawson," he said.

"Thanks for taking a moment, Senator."

Eric had set up the meeting under the guise of him updating top leadership on the investigation. Lambert gestured a hand toward two leather guest chairs next to a leather sofa. "Have a seat, please. I'm eager to hear how the investigation is going."

Eric sat on the sofa while Lambert joined him in a chair.

"So what can you tell me?" Lambert asked, seeming genuinely interested. "Everyone around here is shaking heads at the news of this Turkish assassin guy. The Caracal? It feels right out of a Hollywood movie or something."

"We're making progress, sir."

"Great. How can I help? Carson was a friend. This is all so tragic."

Eric knew that was a lie. Lambert and Carson hated each other.

"We're chasing down every possible lead right now. And one has come up on my radar involving you that I need to speak with you about."

"Me?"

"Yes, sir. Not directly, of course."

"Good to know I'm not a suspect." Lambert laughed. "You want a drink?"

"No, sir. I'm on duty."

"Right. You mind if I do?"

"Not at all."

Lambert stood and walked to a bar cabinet in the corner. He poured himself a glass of what looked like scotch. He took a sip and then returned. But this time he hovered instead of sitting again.

"So what are we talking about?" Lambert asked.

"Mark Edmonds, Senator Carson's chief of staff."

"I like Mark. Tried to recruit him to my team once. But he's always been fiercely loyal to Carson. Something I can certainly appreciate. What about him?"

"We have key information Mark Edmonds was potentially involved in a scheme against you. We have a source who claims Edmonds paid a high-priced call girl to entrap you on the night of April eleventh of this year at the St. Regis hotel here in DC."

He watched Lambert closely. The senator's jaw dropped.

"Entrap me? What are you suggesting?"

"The woman lured you into a private sexual encounter."

His eyes widened. "You can't be serious."

"Unfortunately, I am. We've already verified you were at the hotel that night."

"So what? I sometimes stay there. This is ridiculous. I've been happily married for twenty-five years. I have two beautiful daughters. I would never do this."

"I understand that—"

Lambert continued, interrupting. "I have never once been accused of improper relations with a female other than my wife. This is outrageous."

Eric knew that was another lie. There had been three other accusations over the years. All kept secret and privately handled. He had done his homework.

"Look, Senator. I don't care about your private life. That's your business. I only care if this situation is somehow connected to my investigation."

"So, what . . . you're suggesting I had my friend Lowell Carson killed because his chief of staff was trying to blackmail me?"

"Did you?" Eric boldly asked.

Lambert's eyes went to slits. "Do you know who you're messing with, Agent Dawson? I can make one call and have you removed from this investigation. I'm personal friends with Director Jennings. Don't mess with me."

"I'm not trying to mess with you, sir. I just want the truth."

"You think I'm the only politician Carson used his dirty tricks on? That bastard constantly set up traps around this city. Half of the Senate is probably glad he's dead."

Eric sat up straighter. That felt like an omission of guilt—at least on the sexual encounter with the woman at the St. Regis.

"I welcome any evidence you're willing to submit."

But Lambert was no longer listening to him. "Who put you up to this?"

"No one, sir. I just needed to have this conversation."

"Consider it had. Now get the hell out of my office."

FORTY

The cab stopped in Dupont Circle.

April paid, got out. Even though it was snowing, Dupont Circle managed to attract a small crowd. She was thankful for that. It would be easier to get lost. She bundled herself up tightly, walked to the fountain. She casually surveyed the various people, circled the fountain, then sat on a bench and watched the snow fall for a few minutes.

She got up, headed north up Connecticut Avenue. She'd been on these exact streets before, during a law school function in the city. She remembered the museums, the important international clubs, and the famous historic buildings all around her. She couldn't identify them now, but she admired the different structures. Sidewalk traffic was light. She made sure to keep a watchful eye behind her. She took mental snapshots of random faces just in case they popped up again somewhere else.

She continued to walk. She rubbed her hands together to keep them warm. She passed a man she thought she'd noticed earlier by the fountain. He smiled at her. She did not return the smile, just walked even faster. She glanced behind her, checking on the fountain dude. Thankfully, he wasn't there. She exhaled, crossed the street, spotted several embassies on both sides of the street. Turkey. Sudan. Greece. Even the Bahamas. She thought how nice it would be to fly off to the

Bahamas right now. Maybe she could knock on the door and ask for asylum. *Please take me back to paradise with you.*

She walked two blocks up Connecticut Avenue. She headed north, where the sidewalks were much busier. There were several boutiques, bookstores, and restaurants. She ducked into a café, ordered herself a large cappuccino, found an empty table. She took a seat, watched the front door, tried to call Trisha Sullivan again. Still no answer. She hung up, said her twentieth silent prayer in the past hour. *Please let her be alive.* It was shocking to even have the thought that Edward Sullivan's wife might be in danger. But then someone had ransacked their DC home. She got on her phone and continued to search for Trisha's sister. She found several photos of the two women on Trisha's Instagram account, but it didn't appear that her sister personally did social media. So there was no tagging her and no mention of her sister's last name. Trisha only called her Bonnie in her posts. April had been going bank by bank in the DC area, trying to examine team profile pages to find the woman. It was tedious. There were hundreds of financial institutions. But April had no other way forward. If anyone knew the whereabouts of Trisha Sullivan, it had to be her sister. She found her on the eighty-seventh listing in her search. Bonnie Evers. National Capitol Bank. Pennsylvania Avenue. Vice president, relationship manager. The woman on the profile was a match.

April bolted from the café and flagged a cab at the corner.

FORTY-ONE

Senator Lambert waited twenty minutes without moving from his office window.

His heart was still racing in his chest. He thought if he moved that he might have a heart attack and die on the spot. He was in great physical shape, but this might be too much for any man's heart. When he finally started breathing semi-normally again, he dismissed the few staff members who had remained in the office suite, who looked at him curiously, wondering if he was okay. He reassured them that he was fine. Just exhausted from a very long day. He locked the door to his office, sat down in his leather executive chair. This whole thing was unraveling around him, and he wasn't sure how he could stop it now. He could see that from the look in the FBI agent's eyes. This was not going away anytime soon. No, they were just getting started.

Their ironclad plan had gotten screwed up from the beginning—as soon as some asshole law partner faked his death and began a blackmail scheme that went haywire. At that point, they should have pulled the plug on the whole thing. Called off the dogs and waited. But they didn't. They went forward. They were desperate. He was stupid. And now the whole thing was about to come crashing down on top of him. Lambert grabbed his bottle of scotch off the shelf behind him, poured himself a glass, and then took it down in one gulp. It stung his throat and felt good. His palms were sweaty. He wiped them on the front of his dress pants. But they just kept sweating profusely. Maybe a heart attack wouldn't be such a bad thing. Save him from the humiliation.

This was now about political survival. Every man for himself. He had privately created a contingency plan, his own plan B emergency escape, just in case something like this happened, praying to God that he would never have to use it. But now he wasn't sure he had a choice. He would not and could not take the fall for this thing. He could not let this destroy everything he'd worked his whole life to build. His legacy. He thought about his plan B. He would anonymously point the investigation in a new direction, at a different but legitimate target, at a man everyone would believe was behind the whole thing. As soon as the FBI began to investigate it, they'd find more. Because there was truly so much more there. Lambert would retreat into the hills and weather the storm until it was over. He couldn't lose that battle. They had been so careful. They were clean.

His head was pounding. Power makes you do foolish things. It clouds your head like a dangerous drug and warps your mind. Like a cancer, it changes you from the inside out. And it can quickly bring you to your knees. Lambert picked up his cell phone off his desk, punched a speed-dial button. He could feel the sweat dripping down his cheeks. His left cheek felt numb. Was he having a stroke? The phone rang twice, and then his only trusted friend in the world picked up on the other end. Andrew Rainer. They'd been through hell and back a dozen times already over the past decade. But this latest event was like wrestling with the devil himself. It was time to end this and run for the hills.

"How'd it go?" Rainer asked.

"Not good. We're in serious trouble. Prepare to release the package we put together. It's time to go to plan B. We need to get out before it's too late."

FORTY-TWO

In the warehouse near the airport back in Austin, a surveillance tech recorded the phone conversation. They'd only recently been able to get inside the senator's office suite, his home, and his car. Their client had demanded it. Everyone was paranoid. No one trusted anybody. The tech immediately compressed it into a digital file and emailed it up the chain of command. He wasn't paid to think, but even the lowly security tech knew this wasn't good. Perhaps their powerful client had reason to be paranoid.

FORTY-THREE

The National Capitol Bank was a five-story redbrick building in Capitol Hill. April arrived just before closing and asked to see Bonnie Evers. She waited in the lobby a few minutes and then watched as a woman who matched the online profile came walking out from the back toward her. Bonnie looked a lot like her sister, although with dark hair and a few more wrinkles in her face. She wore a black pantsuit. April stood to greet her as she approached.

"Ms. Ashworth?" Bonnie said.

April had given a fake name. She had no idea what Trisha had told her sister, if anything, and certainly didn't want to spook her before they ever got started.

"Yes, hello. Thanks for seeing me."

"Yes, of course. I'm told you're considering moving your business over and joining us here at National Capitol."

"Correct. I've heard good things."

"Wonderful. Let's talk in my office. Follow me."

April trailed the woman around a corner and entered a spacious office. Bonnie sat behind her desk while April took a guest chair in front.

"What kind of business do you own?" Bonnie asked.

April had no plans to keep up the facade. She got straight to the point. "I don't own a business. That's not why I'm here. I'm looking for your sister, Trisha."

April watched closely to read the eyes of the woman. She was operating under the belief that Bonnie would know what was happening with her sister right now. That Trisha would not have come all the way to DC and not told her sister everything. If that wasn't true, April wasn't sure what to do next. There was a quick flash in Bonnie's eyes. Then it was gone. But it was enough. She knew.

She acted confused. "Trisha?"

"Yes, your sister, Trisha Sullivan."

"Oh, well, she lives in Austin. Why're you looking for her?"

"She's in danger. I think you know that. I'm here to help her."

"I don't know what you're talking about. Who are you?"

"April North. I've been trying to find her for the past twenty-four hours. But she's not answering her phone. You have to help me, Bonnie. Trisha was the one who reached out to my friend Ben Dawson. I know this is about Jerry Dawson."

"I think you need to leave."

"I'm not leaving until you tell me where she is."

"I'll let you discuss this with security."

Bonnie reached for her phone, but April stopped her. "Okay, wait. Listen to me. Here is my phone number." She grabbed a pen and notepad from the desktop and scribbled it down. "If you care about your sister, you'll give this to her. I need to find her immediately. It could save her life. And mine. I'm begging you."

FORTY-FOUR

The beard was gone. He was clean-shaven. The hair was cropped short and now very white. The spectacles had returned. But different from any glasses shown on American television today. Yusuf Demir was traveling as Theodore Lefebvre of Canada. He always immediately changed identities after a kill. He would be changing regularly now that the pesky media was blasting old pictures of him all over their annoying cable news channels. It was an irritation. But it was also a thrill. He enjoyed the challenge of traveling around in this country under such tight scrutiny. It had been some time since he'd worked under this amount of intense pressure. The adrenaline felt good.

He was thirty thousand feet in the air, on his way to Washington, DC. The flight had televisions in each of the seats. He was monitoring CNN. The screen showed a picture of him with a reddish beard and sideburns. Demir remembered the look from a job in Prague six years ago. He'd been captured exiting a car on the Prague subway. Dumb mistake. He'd lost sight of one of the security cameras. It still gnawed at him. He hated mistakes. In a slight Quebec French accent, he asked his neighbor, a dull fortysomething accountant from Texas, what he thought of all this assassin talk on the television. The accountant just shook his head, said he thought that stuff only happened in a John

Grisham novel or in the movies. What was going on in the world? Demir smiled right along with him. Stupid Americans.

He reached down and pulled a magazine out of his bag. Lionel Messi, the famous sports star, was on the cover. Demir had personally seen Messi and the Argentinians win the FIFA World Cup in 2022. A crazy French millionaire had actually wanted the Caracal to kill the legendary player. He declined. Ridiculous what people would pay him millions to do. Just for fun, he told the French millionaire that he would kill any man who tried to have the sports legend eliminated.

He set his phone down in the middle of the magazine and pulled up a photo on the screen. A man in his late forties. Dark hair with some gray. Good-looking. Distinguished. Senator Ted Lambert. There was more information in an encrypted file. He would review it later. His client was willing to pay him whatever he asked on this new assignment, so he just kept milking the cow. But Demir thought, when this was over, he'd take a couple of years off. He could sail his boat around the Mediterranean and visit his many girlfriends. Enjoy life a little. He knew he couldn't stay gone too long. He'd miss the thrill too much.

FORTY-FIVE

April met Dean at the Morrison-Clark Historic Inn, an old Victorian mansion that now served as a hotel in downtown Washington, DC, near the convention center. The hotel was nearly booked. He could only get a second-floor suite with a living room and a separate bedroom. April began to explain her trip over to Bonnie Evers's bank earlier and their uneasy conversation. She was convinced Bonnie knew where Trisha was hiding. She left the phone number along with a desperate plea. Now all they could do was sit tight.

"We can't wait forever," Dean said. "Not with the info we're pulling together."

"Tell me."

Dean had spent the past half hour on the phone with Harvey. "Senator Lambert is the ranking member on the Senate Committee on Energy and Natural Resources. The same committee investigating the gulf oil-spill disaster. The same committee that Hossle Jester, and many other powerful oil executives, were dragged in front of to testify earlier this year, in hopes of avoiding severe penalties and future restrictions that could cost them hundreds of billions of dollars. If it goes bad for them, some of these guys could lose everything, including Jester. Lambert is currently in a key position of influence."

"Billions of dollars of influence."

"But I'm not sure yet what he's getting in return."

"Or how this all ties back to your father."

Every mention of his father brought the possibility of him still being alive right back in front of Dean. It didn't seem real. He had a hard time allowing himself to believe it. He didn't want to be crushed emotionally all over again. Still, everything inside of him wanted to believe if they could somehow solve this mystery, his father would be waiting somewhere on the other side of it.

"That's why we need Trisha Sullivan."

"She's going to call. I can feel it."

Dean collapsed on the sofa in the living room with a sigh. "The FBI came looking for me today. Harvey said agents stopped by the office. He told them I was on vacation."

"What? Why? How do they know about you?"

"My guess is they connected me to Sally Kimble."

"Does the FBI know about me?" April asked, eyes widening.

"Not sure. But now we know why Eric has been blowing up my phone. He knows I'm involved. One way or another, we're working on a limited time frame."

"She'll call. I just know it."

"Keep on repeating that."

FORTY-SIX

The Caracal wondered if he'd ever had an easier target.

Senator Ted Lambert rented a townhome on Capitol Hill, a four-block walk to his office next to the Capitol Building. It was his temporary home while working in Washington, DC. He obviously split time between Florida and his work in this city. The senator was not protected by a governmental security force, unlike American governors and presidents, although many senators chose to hire out private security details. However, this week, because of what happened in Austin, every US senator and congressman was being protected by FBI agents. This information was in the encrypted file.

Standing under the shadow of a tree on a sidewalk across from a block of colorful townhomes, Demir had watched Lambert enter his place through the front door about twenty minutes ago. It was a few minutes before midnight. Lambert had worked very late. Demir had considered killing the senator in his official Senate office, just for the sheer spectacle of it all, wanting to see it on the news, but he wised up and chose the safer and more assured route. This was not the time for a mistake.

Demir glanced up and down the street. It was a quiet, nice neighborhood. He spotted one walker out with a dog across the way. No police cars. He'd walked the sidewalks twice already, checking parked cars, making sure his information was right. The two FBI agents sat clueless in a black Lincoln along the curb. He'd been within five feet of them. He'd even exchanged a glance and nod with one of them.

He checked his watch. There were still lights on in the windows of Lambert's townhome. One of the FBI agents got out to circle the block, as he had every hour on the hour. He disappeared around the corner. He saw the second agent put his cell phone to his ear inside the Lincoln.

Demir stepped away from the tree, crossed the quiet street, slipped through an alley between the townhouses. In the shadows, he calmly walked up the steps to the back door. He pulled a metal tool out of his pocket, moved in close to the door, had it unlocked twenty seconds later. He was silently inside, door shut behind him. There was an alarm. He typed in the code. The console light went from red to green. Through a high-powered lens, he'd watched through the front window as Lambert had typed in the same code earlier. He heard a TV on in the living area up the hallway. But he heard no movement anywhere else inside the two-story townhome.

Wearing surgical gloves, Demir pulled out his Ruger Mark 11 revolver with silencer from his jacket pocket. He stepped carefully forward, light on his feet. A wolf approaching his prey. French doors to the living area were five feet ahead. They were cracked. He could tell immediately the TV was on a news channel he liked. He recognized the voice of the sexy anchor. Demir peered carefully around the door opening. He smiled. Senator Lambert was sitting in a leather recliner, legs up, eyes closed, a glass of scotch spilled on his lap in front of him. He looked passed out. Demir turned to the TV screen when he heard his name. He smiled again. How ironic. The beautiful redheaded anchor was talking about him at this very moment. And he was about to create even more dramatic international news. What a great life. He put the gun within two feet of Lambert's temple and pulled the trigger. Lambert jerked but barely moved. Demir pulled the trigger again. Same spot. Blood began flowing down the senator's neck. Demir watched for just a moment. The man was gone.

The gun was back in his pocket, and he was out the back door. Seconds later, he was on the front sidewalk, strolling, hands in his pockets. He crossed paths with the second agent who had circled the block as a protective measure.

"Good evening," Demir said.

"Evening," replied the agent.

Stupid FBI. The Caracal smiled.

FORTY-SEVEN

Back in Austin, Eric was sleeping on a cheap sofa in a small lounge outside his office when Brewster suddenly barged in and flipped on the lights.

"Boss!" Brewster said.

Eric checked his watch. A few minutes after six in the morning. "What the hell?"

"Sorry, but you won't believe this. Senator Lambert is dead."

Eric bolted straight up. "What? How?"

"Shot in the head at close range inside his Capitol Hill townhome during the night. DC had two of our boys parked out front the entire night. Never saw anything. Went to check on him just now when one of his staffers showed up at the place, said he'd missed an early appointment and wasn't answering his phone. They found the senator still sitting in his recliner in front of the TV, dried-up blood on his face and puddled on the carpet beneath him, a crater in the man's temple."

Eric cursed. "Self-inflicted?"

"No, sir. This was a professional kill."

Eric felt a migraine forming. He stood, grimaced from an immediate ache in his back, his mind already reliving every word of his conversation with Senator Lambert the previous day. Had someone been listening? Did the FBI's sudden appearance in the senator's office and

Eric's aggressive questions send up warning signals that had pushed a panic button somewhere? Who could have killed him? He thought of Yusuf Demir. Was it possible he had been the one to pull the trigger? Eric had walked out of his meeting with Lambert yesterday suspecting the man had a connection to Carson's assassination. But a bullet to his head had just confirmed it.

"Sir, it gets worse," Brewster said. "The press is already there."

FORTY-EIGHT

Her phone beeped and buzzed. April shot straight up in bed.

She knocked the phone to the floor from the nightstand while trying to frantically grab it, then quickly scrambled from under the covers to the carpet. It beeped and buzzed again. She found it. It was a text message. She looked at the clock: 7:07. She felt fuzzy-headed and still tired. She and Dean had stayed up past two in the morning trying to decide what to do next since Trisha was clearly never going to get in touch with them. The text message was from an unidentified DC phone number. It was different from the original number she'd had for Trisha Sullivan.

Text one: Can we meet this morning, April?

Text two: Trisha

April replied: Yes! Please! Just say when and where.

Union Station. Cava. 10am.

I'll be there!

April felt her heart racing. She'd given up hope. She wanted to immediately call the woman, beg her to start talking on the phone, and help them find out the truth. She didn't want any more delays or to take any further chances. But she also wanted to respect Trisha's choice of communication. If the woman wanted to talk on the phone, she would have called. But waiting the next three hours might be painful. She turned on the lamp, walked into the living room, found Dean asleep with one leg hanging off the sofa and the other bent awkwardly beneath him. She smiled and felt sorry for him. The sofa looked so uncomfortable. She had no idea how her time with Dean would conclude after this was all over—if they lived through it. Walking away from him the first time had been the hardest thing she'd ever done. She wasn't sure she could survive doing it a second time. That was why she'd had her guard up the past couple of days. She couldn't fall in love with him all over again. But something told her it might already be too late. Dean was snoring something fierce and was obviously not struggling to find a REM cycle, unlike her. She knelt next to him, touched his shoulder.

Dean whipped around. "What? You okay? What is it?"

"I just got a text from Trisha. We're on for this morning."

This instantly stirred him fully awake. "When?"

"Union Station at ten."

"Hallelujah."

April turned around to glance at the TV. Dean had fallen asleep with it still on and the volume low. A breaking-news alert was on the screen.

"Dean!" she gasped.

He sat up and joined her in watching the stunning news. Senator Ted Lambert was dead. Killed by gunshot in his DC townhome the previous night by an intruder. Suspect still at large. FBI involved. Few details at this point.

"What does this mean?" April asked.

"It means we're close to the truth."

FORTY-NINE

They settled in at a small table at CAVA, a casual Mediterranean restaurant, on the ground level of Union Station. It was situated right off the opulent Main Hall. From the table, they had a good view of their surroundings. Union Station was already packed with shoppers, eaters, and travelers. Dean took a quick moment to marvel at the enormity of the famous old train station. They ordered coffee, sat close together, both of them filled with nerves. It felt like such a pivotal moment. Would Trisha show? Was his father still alive? Did his dad still have something left to say?

"What happens if she skips out on us?" April asked, tapping her fingernails on the table.

"Then I keep looking. And you get on a plane to Europe today."

"Yeah, sure."

"I'm serious, April. There are only so many times we can get away from them. Our luck will run out eventually. These guys have proven to be relentless. I'm still uneasy about FBI protection. The only other option is for you to skip town."

"So I go tour the Eiffel Tower while you dodge bullets?"

"Exactly."

"Not a chance. I'm a big girl. I'm seeing this all the way to the end with you."

He shook his head. "You really are the most stubborn person I've ever known."

"You should be used to it by now."

He fiddled with his coffee cup. "Then I guess we keep fighting and clawing until we're completely out of options. Fred, my boss's boss, is right. This story is already huge without directly connecting all these pieces."

April considered that. "You think it's enough to drive the bad guys into hiding? Give us a safe reprieve?"

"I don't know. But I could give Eric everything we've gathered. And hope it would be enough for them to start arresting people."

"Maybe. But we really need Trisha to show."

Dean looked out into the Main Hall, where shoppers and travelers zigzagged through the busy section. He searched the faces for Trisha Sullivan. At the same time, he watched for signs of any suspicious eyes staring back at them. Someone had been to Trisha's DC home yesterday. Someone was already on her trail. Could they be inside Union Station right now? It was hard to track. There were hundreds of people in the Main Hall. They sat there fidgeting while the clock clicked past 10:15. April sent a quick text to the phone number. No response. Dean thought he noticed a man staring at them from across the way. He sat on a bench with a book in his hands. But his eyes kept popping up. This made him nervous. He felt vulnerable. Could this be a setup to lure them out in the open? He was getting ready to suggest they walk when April spotted her.

"She's here," she said, glancing over his shoulder.

Dean turned. Trisha Sullivan walked quickly across the Main Hall in their direction. She wore a gray coat, a maroon scarf, and hid her eyes behind big black sunglasses. But it was her. Dean was sure of it. They both stood and April hurried over to meet her. She shared a quick hug with Trisha, since they knew each other, and then pointed back at Dean. Trisha looked over at him, nodded, likely agreeing it was okay he was there. The two women joined him by the table. Trisha said she felt like she already knew him because of everything his father had told her about him. It felt surreal to hear her say that, not even knowing the nature of her relationship with his dad.

They all sat down.

"Thank you for coming," April said.

"I'm sorry I didn't respond to you sooner, April," Trisha said. "It has been a horrible few days for me. I've been scared to death. Honestly, I wasn't sure if I could trust you. I mean, you work with my husband. And he can't know about any of this. But after you came to see my sister at the bank yesterday, I knew we had to talk."

"You can trust us. We're also scared. For many of the same reasons."

She removed the sunglasses, showing bloodshot eyes.

"Are you okay?" April asked. "I mean, physically, are you okay?"

"Yes. But I'm a train wreck emotionally. Someone ransacked my house here yesterday. I came home to find everything destroyed." She looked over at Dean. "I don't know who did it, but I think it has to do with your father."

"Is my father still alive, Trisha?" Dean said, the question he'd been dying to ask from the moment she'd walked up to them.

She swallowed. "I don't know, Dean. He was alive up until three days ago. But I haven't heard anything from him since."

Dean felt adrenaline shoot through him. It was one thing to speculate that his father had not died in the boating incident. But it was another thing to hear her confirm it. He felt like he'd just put on an oxygen mask after struggling to breathe for the past couple days. "Where is he?"

"Costa Rica. At least, that's where he's been hiding the past few months."

Dean tilted his head. "Were you guys . . . together?"

Trisha sighed. "Yes. I have so much to tell you. I don't even know where to start."

"When did things begin between you and Jerry?" April asked.

"A year ago. My husband became abusive with me after a few years of us being married. It started emotionally but then grew to be physical. Edward can be a very domineering person, as you probably know. Jerry began to notice some markings on my face when we were around each other at dinner functions. I just confided in him, at first, trying to get some emotional support. But it quickly grew from there."

"Did anyone else know about it?" April asked.

"No one. Not even my sister. Look, I'm not proud of the affair, okay?"

"We're not here to judge you," April reassured her. "We're just trying to get to the truth. This is much bigger than your relationship with Jerry."

"What is going on? How is it bigger?"

As they'd discussed, April handled most of the dialogue. "If we're going to get you out of this, I need you to be completely honest with me. We need to know everything about your and Jerry's relationship and what you did together."

"Fine." She nodded without a fight. "I'm sick of hiding it."

"What was your plan with Jerry?"

"I was supposed to join him in Costa Rica in about three months. After he felt confident things had settled, and we were okay. I love him. And I was willing to do anything to be with him. We were going to buy a boat with a full staff and sail around the world. See exotic places. Live a fantasy life, is what Jerry kept telling me."

Dean leaned forward. "Where did the money you invested with J. Walter Petroleum come from?"

"Mostly from me. Jerry had a little stashed away. I cashed out some old family investments without my husband knowing about it."

"Jerry came up with the plan?" he said.

"Yes, of course. I'm not half as smart as your father. He said he had a way to turn a few million dollars into more than twenty million nearly overnight. Something that would last us the rest of our lives together."

"Then he faked his own death?" Dean asked.

Trisha nodded. "I was concerned how that would impact you and your brothers, but Jerry said he had no other options. Even though he hated it, he said his hand had been forced. Jerry asked me to trust him. Which I did. He said things had to go down this way. He said something bad was happening at the firm and he didn't want any part of it. But he already knew too much about certain things, so he would never be allowed to simply walk away. He was dealing with dangerous people. But he was done with it. He had to get out. So he dreamed up this extravagant plan. I told him I didn't care about the money. That we could just disappear together. But Jerry wanted the best life for us. He wanted to be able to take me all over the world, to drink the finest wines and stay in the best hotels. That was your dad. He was an idealist and such a romantic."

Dean considered that. His father had never been good with money. He lived an over-the-top lifestyle. Cars, homes, clothes, vacations. So he was not surprised his dad didn't just walk away with a couple million. If he had, they would probably be in Costa Rica together right now without any concerns. But he went for the big catch. And that was likely why their plans had unraveled on them.

"Did my dad ever mention the name 'Hossle Jester' to you? Or 'Senator Lambert'?"

"Yes. Not many details. Just that they were bad characters and the reason he had to leave the firm the way he did. But my husband started to ask questions about my family funds and recent travel schedule. I think he may have started to figure out I was involved with Jerry. Which is why I bolted from Austin yesterday." She reached into her purse, pulled out a business card, and handed it to Dean. "Before he left, Jerry gave this to me. He told me if anything happened to him, I should give it to you. You would know what to do with it."

Dean examined it. It was his father's business card from Michaels & Peterson. He flipped it over to the back. He recognized his dad's neat print handwriting. His father had written down an address for a UPS Store in Austin. A mailbox number. And an entry code. Dean felt chill bumps cover his arms. His father had left something behind. What? It had to be something significant. They had to get back to Austin ASAP.

"What do I do now?" Trisha asked.

"Do you have somewhere safe you can hide?" April said.

"Maybe. Jerry and I had a secret little condo off 30A in Florida. He purchased it through some company he owned. It was just our little getaway. We would sneak away there for a couple days at a time. I could go there and hide out."

"Go there," Dean insisted. "Leave straight from here. We will reach back out to you when we think it's safe."

They all stood together to say their goodbyes. That was when Dean spotted him standing in front of a store fifty feet away. There was something familiar about him. Mid-thirties. Clean-cut. Jeans. Denim jacket. When the guy made direct eye contact with him, Dean confirmed it. Buick Boy. The same guy who had been parked outside Trisha's townhome yesterday. Had he followed Trisha here this morning? Or could he have trailed them? Didn't matter. Dean knew they just had to get rid of him. He tried to remain calm. He didn't want to panic Trisha. The woman was already unsteady. From the corner of his eye, he scanned the rest of the concourse. Were there others out there? His palms began to sweat. He couldn't be sure.

He leaned into April's ear, whispered, "Hey, let's split up. Make sure Trisha gets into a car and gets out of here. I'll meet you in front in a few minutes."

She turned. "Why?"

"Trust me."

He could see April wanted a better answer than that. But Trisha was watching, so she didn't fight him on it.

"Let me walk you out," she said to Trisha.

As April and Trisha moved down the Main Hall, Dean peeled off in another direction. He took a quick peek over his shoulder. Buick Boy was also on the move. Then he noticed the guy speak into his hand. Dean cursed. There were others. How many? And where? Dean headed toward the down escalator. Buick Boy followed. That was good. Dean knew April and Trisha were safe from at least this one guy. Dean took the escalator down to the lower level toward the food court. It was busy. Lots of people at tables eating cheap breakfast food. He briskly walked past the tables and chairs. Another glance behind him. Buick Boy was matching his pace, hands in his pockets. Dean wondered if anything else was in his pocket. A gun? Dean suddenly stopped. Another guy appeared in front of him at thirty feet. Dark beard, hunting jacket. There was no mistaking that the man was there for him. His eyes were locked in on Dean. Who the hell were these guys? Were they going to try to grab him in public?

Dean wasn't going to hang around to find out. He immediately bolted to his right, cut through a pack of diners, around tables. Both men reacted in pursuit. They were coming after him. Were there others currently going after April? He needed to get back to her to find out. He rushed forward, his tennis shoes slapping down on the shiny floor. People turned to stare at the man who was suddenly running inside the mall. Dean accidentally knocked over a guy who stepped into his path. They both went sprawling to the floor, which caused more commotion. Now everyone was staring. Dean got to his feet, ran up ahead, found the escalator back up to the ground level. His two chasers were in close pursuit. Dean pushed around other people on the escalator, drawing the ire and curses of many. He reached the top, back on ground level, and went into an all-out sprint across the Main Hall. Dean spotted a security guard in uniform up ahead of him. Instead of trying to avoid him, Dean ran straight toward him.

When he was within ten feet, Dean pointed behind him and yelled as loud as he could, "He's got a gun!"

This sent a ripple of panic into the crowd. Which was what he'd intended. People began ducking and scrambling like mad for exits. The security guard drew his weapon. Dean spun around to watch his two followers. Both men looked at each other as if trying to decide what to do and then peeled off in opposite directions. Neither man was still in pursuit of him. The security guard held a walkie-talkie to his lips, started yelling some kind of emergency code into it. Dean didn't hang around to see what happened next. He located an exit door in a crowd of others, hit the sidewalk.

He found April safely waiting for him a couple minutes later.

FIFTY

Dean rented a car at a Hertz station nearby, and they left the city as swiftly as possible. Trisha was safe. For now. April had put her in a taxi and watched her drive away. They both hoped she remained that way. They were concerned about using any of the Washington, DC, airports now that they'd been identified in the city. So Dean drove the rental car south, away from the city, headed toward the Richmond International Airport. It would add two hours to their journey home, but April admitted it would make her feel much safer to get on a plane somewhere else. Anywhere else.

Dean spent a good portion of his time on his cell phone talking with Harvey. Fred was about to go berserk. The news out of DC that Senator Lambert had been assassinated only added more fuel to the fire. News was breaking everywhere, and they were missing the boat. Fred heard a rumor that *The New York Times* was sitting on something explosive. An FBI insider who said they had a video of Lambert with a prostitute. And that someone on Carson's staff had used it to blackmail the senator. Everyone in the newsroom was waiting around on pins and needles. Waiting for him to get his ass back home. Dean promised Harvey that unless the *Times* reporter was sitting in a condo with the Caracal himself, they couldn't touch the angle they were currently working. They would be home soon and would need to make one more quick stop. Then they could not only satisfy Fred's every anxiety but also help bring justice to the situation.

"How's April?" Harvey asked.

Dean glanced over. April was asleep with her head propped against the window. "She's amazing, Harvey. In her position, I probably wouldn't have the same fortitude. She insists on seeing this all the way through. I'm not sure I'd do the same."

"Well, you keep your head in the game until this is over."

"I'm trying." Dean smiled. "What time is our flight, boss?"

Harvey had booked them two seats out of Richmond on the next available flight.

"One forty."

Dean glanced at the clock on the rental car. "We should just make it."

"I'll pick you up at the airport. Don't miss the flight, Dean. Or Fred will have a stroke."

"Yes, boss."

"There is one more interesting thing, Dean."

"What's that?"

"Your friend Hossle Jester will be at a fundraiser for Ballet Austin in downtown tonight. His wife is on the board. I confirmed the guest list."

"Really? Maybe I'll pay him a visit."

"Just get home. Now."

"Yes, sir."

Dean hung up, pushed down even farther on the gas pedal. April stirred with the sudden jolt of the vehicle. She looked over at him with sleepy eyes.

"Hey," he said.

"Where are we?"

"Forty minutes out. You passed out almost mid-sentence a while back."

"I'm so tired. I feel like I haven't slept in more than a week."

"This is almost over."

"I hope you're right."

"What will you do, April? When this is all done."

"What do you mean?"

"Will you still practice law?"

"I don't know. I haven't really thought about it. I guess things are probably going to change quite a bit around my law firm."

"Yes, I would imagine. That place might get shut down completely by the feds if we prove it was connected to both Carson's and Lambert's deaths."

"Fine by me. I'm done with it."

"Have you ever wanted to do something else? Other than practice law?"

She glanced out the window, a small grin touching her lips. "Yes, but I was too scared to even try. Just felt whimsical. Even though my father always encouraged me."

"What did you want to do?"

"Be a travel writer. See the world, chronicle my experiences, submit them to magazines."

Dean smiled. "Sounds wonderful. Now might be a great time to give it a go."

"And what about you? What will you do when this is over?"

He wanted to say he'd quit while he was ahead and travel the globe with the gorgeous brunette sitting in the passenger seat. But he couldn't get himself to say it. And she hadn't invited him yet. "I don't know. I guess I'll do what any good journalist does. Move on to the next story."

But he wasn't sure he wanted to move on.

Not if April was on the other side of the world without him.

FIFTY-ONE

Their flight left Richmond without incident. A few stares, but Dean thought they were just the casual glances of men wanting to catch a better look at the gal next to him. Especially since none of them were paying any attention to him. When the plane hit the air, they both breathed a little bit easier. April again slept on the plane. Dean began jotting down outlines on napkins and sorting everything out, trying to figure out the best way to connect the dots. It was a fantastical tale with a lot of great characters and incredible intrigue. But there was a big hole in the middle of the story. He really needed his father to fill in the holes for him and connect Hossle Jester to Senator Lambert. He thought about his dad. The man had not died in the boating incident. But if he'd been tracked down in Costa Rica by dangerous players, was he even still alive? If so, how would Dean find him? This was definitely where he'd need Eric's help.

The plane touched down in Austin. They traveled without luggage. They'd left their clothes back at the hotel in Washington. They weren't risking going back for them. While April made a quick restroom pit stop inside, Dean hit the sidewalk and looked for Harvey. His editor was right on time. He pulled up to the curb in his white Grand Cherokee. However, Dean immediately spotted the black Ford sedan pull up directly behind him, only a few feet away. Two men in dark suits and shades jumped out, rushed toward Dean. They were not killers. He could tell they were cops. Feds. Dean cursed. Their appearance seemed to surprise even his editor, who paused while getting out of his vehicle and stared back and forth at Dean and the FBI agents. His editor's face said everything. *Crap!* The feds must have followed him without his knowledge.

"Don't say anything," Harvey instructed. "I'll get our attorney on it."

"Dean Dawson?" one of the men demanded, five feet away.

"Nope," he replied. "My name is Jose Hernandez."

They weren't amused. Clearly they knew who he was. They both flipped badges in near unison. "FBI, Mr. Dawson. We need a word with you, sir."

"I'm a little busy right now, guys. How about tomorrow morning?"

"You need to come with us right now. It's not a request."

Dean glanced at Harvey, wondering what to do. He did not want April picked up by these guys, too, which was why he decided to not fight this right now. She was still inside. If he left quickly with them, they would never know about her. He hoped.

"Okay, boys, lead the way. I'd like to catch up with my brother anyway."

Dean followed the agents. One of them opened the back door of the Explorer, guided him inside. As they pulled away from the curb, Dean spotted April walking out of the building. Harvey immediately rushed over to her. Dean dropped his head back against the leather. He had no idea how he was going to find his way through this now. But he was determined. They were too damn close to the finish line.

FIFTY-TWO

They drove Dean downtown and escorted him into a quiet office suite on the fourth floor of a nondescript building. A room with sofas, chairs, tables, and what looked like a restroom in the corner. The two FBI agents told him he could make himself comfortable, that someone would be in to speak with him shortly. They shut the door behind them, leaving him all alone. He went to the window. No balcony. Although it'd likely be too high for him to jump from anyway. Dean wondered if the room was wired or bugged with audio or video surveillance equipment. To be safe, he huddled inside the restroom by the toilet, door shut, sink water running, and texted April he was okay. He would be out of this mess shortly, not to worry, he'd be in touch. Just hang tight. He got a text back saying she was with Harvey and doing okay.

He sat on the sofa, stared at the wall. He was getting really frustrated with the wait when his brother finally barged into the room. Eric's face was red. He was already angry. Eric had been calling and texting him relentlessly for more than twenty-four hours. Dean understood his frustration. What did Eric and the FBI know? Were they aware of April's involvement? He presumed they weren't, since the two FBI agents who greeted him at the airport didn't hang around searching for his female travel companion earlier. His mind was running in a hundred different directions.

"Your phone broken?" Eric began, standing in front of him, arms crossed.

"Sorry, man. I've been busy."

"So it seems. Why were you meeting with Sally Kimble two nights ago?"

"I can't tell you that. Not yet, at least. I'm sorry."

"Why the hell not?"

"It's, uh . . . complicated. I need more time."

"I need to know what you know, Dean. People's lives are on the line."

Dean thought about April. "Yes, I know. That's why it's complicated."

Eric exhaled heavily. "You're obstructing justice. I can arrest you. You ever spent the night in a jail cell?"

"I once spent the weekend in Cornville, Oklahoma. Does that count?"

"I'm being serious. I could get in trouble for letting you go."

"I'm not trying to put you in a bad spot. I swear. But putting me in a jail cell does neither of us any good right now."

"Why were you in Richmond, Virginia, today?"

"I can't tell you that, either. I need more time."

"I don't think you get it. You're in danger. I'm trying to protect you."

"Look, I appreciate that. I really do. And if you give me a few more hours, I'll tell you everything I know. That's all I'm asking for."

"A few more hours could get you killed."

Dean didn't respond to that. He felt conflicted. He hated keeping things from his brother. He knew the FBI could help in so many ways. But he remained hesitant to place April's safety in their hands. He also wanted to know what his father was hiding in the UPS box. If it was incriminating in some way, Dean wanted to protect his dad. He was in a position to do that. Eric wasn't. Not as an FBI agent. But he needed to give his brother something. Eric deserved that. And Eric gave him the opening with his next question.

"How is Dad's former secretary involved in all of this?"

"Because Dad didn't die on that boat four months ago."

Eric's mouth dropped open. "What?"

"Dad may still be alive, Eric. He faked his death. I'm trying to get to the truth. This is what I've been working on the past couple of days."

"What the hell are you talking about?"

"The woman you told me about who visited Ben the other day wasn't crazy. She was telling the truth. I spoke with her this morning. Dad is probably alive. And believe it or not, his situation connects right back to Carson's assassination three nights ago."

"Is this another one of your reporter games?"

"I'm dead serious. Give me a few hours and I'll prove it."

FIFTY-THREE

Dean refused a courtesy ride from the feds. Instead, he caught a cab outside the building and minutes later was dropped in front of Sun & Fun Boat Rentals along Lake Austin, just a few miles away from the downtown skyline. Dean had called the rental shop on the way over, set everything up. He knew Eric would have his agents try to follow him around town. Part of that was his brother's genuine concern for his safety. Which he appreciated. But he could not allow anyone to follow him right now. Not until he looked in that UPS box. He got out of the cab, hurried into the small boat-rental building. He noticed the same black Explorer pull into the parking lot behind him, as he'd expected. They were not even trying to be discreet. But he saw no other suspicious vehicles. If any bad guys were out there somewhere, he'd yet to spot them. There was no sign of Oscar or Felix. He'd been watching out the windows the entire drive.

Dean signed a few quick forms at the counter inside, then a young guy with a goatee guided him to the pier behind the building, where a Supra Sunsport inboard ski boat was tied up for him. There were several other boats also tied up. Dean climbed aboard. The guy with the goatee untied the ski boat, gave him a few last-minute instructions, and Dean backed out into the water. He had grown up on boats because one of his childhood buddies' parents owned one. He was comfortable in the driver's seat. He looked over his shoulder and smiled when he noticed the FBI boys in the black suits sprinting up to the pier as if they'd just put together what was going down in front of them. Real geniuses. They flashed badges at Mr. Goatee, pointed at another boat, but the kid just shrugged and began arguing with them. Dean had slipped the kid an extra fifty dollars to stall these guys for as long as possible. He only needed a few extra minutes.

Dean pushed the handle forward, floored the gas, and the boat jumped across the ice-cold water. A mile up the river, he found his destination, a dock attached to a boathouse, and parked the boat in a slip, tied it off, and raced up the wooden dock to a street on the other side. Just as planned, a taxi was waiting on the curb. April sat low in the back seat, eyes glued out the window, waiting for him. Dean jumped into the back seat beside her. They shared a quick smile. They were in the clear. For now.

The downtown UPS Store was on the ground floor of the Hilton Austin off Fourth Street. The cab dropped them at the curb. Dean quickly glanced around. Groups of people were everywhere. Work had let out a half hour ago all over downtown. Buildings were emptying onto the sidewalks. It was a good time to get lost in a crowd. They hurried into the building. The UPS Store was off to the side of the plush hotel lobby. Dean grabbed April by the hand, led her through the lobby, into the store. They quickly scoured the rental mailboxes, looking for one that matched up with the information Trisha had given them that morning. When they found it, they both gave each other an anxious look. This was it. They both could feel it. Four days of monitoring secret meetings, evading followers, and being chased around the country had led them to this moment. One way or another, this was the end of the road for them.

Dean typed in the code for the mailbox. He pulled the door open, reached inside, and found an unmarked manila folder. He pulled it from the box.

"Let's go somewhere more private," Dean suggested, shutting the box.

They reentered the hotel lobby, found two leather chairs tucked away in the corner. Dean's heart was pounding. They sat closely together, knees touching, again shared a prayerful look. Dean used his finger to tear open the envelope. Inside, he discovered a thin stack of eight-by-ten color photographs. They looked like secret surveillance photographs taken from a distance. But the faces in the photographs were clear as day. Hossle Jester standing right next to Senator Ted Lambert on a huge boat. Dean flipped to the next image. It showed the name on the back of the boat: *Scorpion Season*. The boat obviously belonged to Hossle Jester. More pictures. Jester and Lambert smiling, laughing together, Lambert with his right arm wrapped around Jester's shoulder. Like they were buddies. This was not a quick, formal meet and greet in the lobby of the Senate Building after Jester had testified on Capitol Hill earlier this year. These were incriminating photos, considering Lambert's position as head of the Senate committee investigating a gulf oil spill with hundreds of billions on the line.

More photos showed other men on the boat. Two of them were Edward Sullivan and Jerry Dawson. Behind the eight-by-ten photographs, Dean found a printed copy of a message exchange between his father, Edward Sullivan, Hossle Jester, and Senator Lambert on an online platform called DarkKnight. Dean presumed it was an encrypted web platform they used to hide their communication. One message from Edward Sullivan included a profile sheet on Yusuf Demir, the legendary Caracal. Sullivan had typed: *Found our guy. Contact has been made. $40 million is the ask.* The send date on the message was two weeks before Dean's father had supposedly died out on Lake Travis.

"Do you think your dad hired someone to take these photos?" April asked.

"That's my guess."

"Then he used them to hijack Lease Sale 151?"

"Probably. My dad didn't want any part of what these men were planning. But he also wasn't satisfied simply walking away. He wanted to get paid. That was stupid."

"But why kill Senator Lambert?"

"Panic, I presume. Their plan was unraveling on them. And maybe the man with billions on the line decided to start eliminating any possible connections to himself. Your boss could be next. And who knows who else."

"That's scary."

"Yeah. And that crazy man is only a half mile from us right now."

April's eyes narrowed. "You want to confront him directly?"

"Yes."

Her mouth dropped open. "Now *you're* being crazy. Why?"

"I watched every minute of his testimony in front of the Senate committee. Hossle Jester hated being questioned by them. You could tell. The veins were bulging in his forehead. It was clear he felt untouchable and wanted to unleash on them. He nearly did several times before his attorneys cut him off. I think if I approach him the right way, I can get him to admit his involvement. That would go a long way toward bringing him to justice before he can hide behind his army of lawyers."

FIFTY-FOUR

Dean and April took an escalator up to the second level of the JW Marriott, where the fundraiser was being held outside on the lush second-story patio. A huge stage had been set up, and a local country band was playing and entertaining a growing crowd of several hundred. Circular tables with white cloths and linens were spread throughout the patio. Strings of white lights were hung everywhere. A line had formed at a buffet, as affluent men and women in black tuxedos and silk and sequined cocktail dresses filled plates with expensive food. Dean spotted several sheriffs-for-hire in their standard tan uniforms with guns at their belts.

There had been nothing but high-dollar Mercedes, BMWs, and Range Rovers pulling through the circular valet in the front of the hotel. They were not dressed for the part, both wearing blue jeans, tennis shoes, and jackets. They were not on the fundraiser invite list, of course, but Harvey had a contact who had gotten them added to the media invite list. Dean had already walked past a couple of TV reporters in the main lobby with cameras in their pretty faces and microphones at their mouths. He also recognized several of the print and online media there to cover the event, already cornering prominent donors.

They entered the massive outdoor patio. Dean scanned every face for the small gray-haired man with the beady eyes named Hossle

Jester. The Scorpion. The man who paid the bill for the Caracal. The man greedy enough to go on an all-out killing spree to protect his insane wealth. The man behind the thick curtain of all this madness. The crowd looked like a who's who of Austin's finest. There were several celebrity actors and sports figures. Dean even spotted Governor McCaffrey standing in the middle, shaking enthusiastic hands with every person who ventured by him, a permanent smile etched onto his tan face, and his wife dolled up in a red dress and glittering diamonds beside him.

"I feel odd being here dressed like this," April said to him.

"Let's just get in and get out. I don't plan to hit the buffet line. Do you see him?"

April peered over the bustling crowd. "Not yet."

They moved through the perfectly decorated circular tables. The band kicked off another country tune. They were indeed getting a few strange stares because of their out-of-place attire. Dean didn't care. He was focused. After all this, he wanted a direct shot at Hossle Jester. He wanted to look pure evil in the eye and ask him for the truth. Something any reporter would do before publishing a story. Then they would get the hell out of there and find protection behind the walls of his newsroom. Harvey and the team were waiting. They were offered drinks by several circling waiters with trays hovering over shoulders but declined. They moved easily through the engaged crowd.

"Dean!" April said suddenly, nodding across the grounds.

Dean turned, spotted him immediately. Hossle Jester wore a simple black tuxedo with a black bow tie. His hair was gray and thinning on top. His face was wrinkled and looked beaten from years under direct sun while out on oil rigs. The eyes were tiny and dark. He stood in a circle with two other gray-haired men in black tuxedos. Jester had a bottle of beer in his frail fingers. Dean felt a rush of nerves wash over him. He thought about the pictures of Jester and Lambert. The sinister deal they must've struck. And all the blood that had been shed because of it. Including Sally Kimble. This was the moment of truth. He was about to be face-to-face with a ruthless killer.

He grabbed April's hand, pulled her across the patio.

Dean's adrenaline was pumping with each step. He was twenty feet away. He spotted a sheriff in uniform ten feet off to his left. A man in a black suit, not a tuxedo, with an earpiece in his left ear, beside the stage to his right. He felt safe. Or at least as safe as he could now that he was within ten feet of this man. Five feet. He wasn't slowing down. It had all come to this moment. Dean swallowed the knot in his throat, stepped directly inside the circle of these powerful men, April standing two feet behind him.

"Good evening, gentlemen," Dean interrupted, all eyes turning to stare. Dean looked straight into the dark eyes of the Scorpion. "Mr. Jester, may I have a word with you, sir?"

Jester's eyes became even smaller. "Who the hell are you?"

"My name is Dean Dawson. I'm a reporter with *TexasNow*."

"Never heard of it," Jester scoffed. "I don't speak to you idiots anyway. Get away from me, son, before I have you thrown out of here. Or worse."

The other two men were staring at their interaction. Dean knew this was his one shot. Jester could indeed have him thrown out with a few quick words. The man with the earpiece ten feet away had perked up. Dean had to strike, and he had to take his best swing at Jester right now. He took a quick breath, gathered himself.

"Mr. Jester, we're running a story tonight that directly connects you to the assassination of Senator Carson. We believe you and Senator Ted Lambert coordinated a secret arrangement to have Carson killed. We believe you hired Yusuf Demir, the assassin the FBI has targeted in their search. We also believe you are behind the assassination of Senator Lambert in Washington, DC, this morning. Now, sir, before we publish this story, would you like to comment?"

The two gray-haired men in the circle were now gawking in shock. There were a few others around who had stopped to listen, and who were standing there with their mouths open. Jester's pale, wrinkled face went red.

"You're out of your damn mind, son. You publish that and I'll own your publication by tomorrow afternoon. Do you have any idea who you're talking to right now?"

"Yes, sir, I do. Are you denying your relationship with Senator Lambert?"

"Of course. Never even met him in person."

Dean reached into his jacket, pulled out one of the eight-by-ten photographs. He held it up for all in the circle to see, the best shot of Jester and Lambert together, smiling, Lambert's arm over the older man's shoulder.

"Care to comment on this photograph, Mr. Jester? This was recently taken on your boat. I have several more of you two enjoying each other's company."

More people were starting to gather around the group, staring wide-eyed, wondering what was going on in this bit of drama in the very corner of the party. Especially with the red-faced old man they knew to be a billionaire making threats to Dean. It was clear this was not a casual conversation. A couple of onlookers had their cell phones out and were recording the encounter.

Jester noticed the stares. Dean spotted a bead of sweat on his wrinkled forehead. "Son, you print these lies and you're a dead man. Do you understand me?"

This caused some mouths to drop open even more.

"Are you threatening me, sir?" Dean asked.

"It's not a threat. You have no idea what I'm capable of."

"I think I do. You've demonstrated that for the whole world this past week."

"What I did to Carson won't compare to what I'm going to do to you."

This got everyone's attention. Dean heard a couple of audible gasps. The man had come right out and said it. While Dean had believed he could entice the hotheaded man into confessing, hearing him actually do it was surreal and stunning. It was time to go. He'd gotten what he'd wanted. No other words were necessary. He needed to write this story and bring the crazy old man to justice. Not only for Carson. But for Sally Kimble.

"Enjoy the party," Dean said.

He turned, grabbed April. "Let's get out of here."

They were crossing the patio at full speed when Dean noticed him. He saw the eyes first. They were the same eyes as the man who'd bumped into him the night of Sally Kimble's death. He was sure of it. Yusuf Demir. Ten feet in front of him. He'd never forget those eyes. And now the assassin was standing directly in front of them. Dean stiffened, stopped April, felt panic rush through him. Demir was wearing a black leather jacket and spectacles. The hair was now jet black with sideburns. Dean's greatest fear was confirmed when Demir suddenly pulled a weapon out from beneath his jacket, aimed directly at them. There was an isolated woman's scream in the air. Dean turned in front of April, put out an arm, a protective instinct. He heard a thud in the air, the trigger of a gun with a silencer, felt something pop in the back of his shoulder, and then pain surge through his whole body. The jolt sent him toppling on top of April as both hit the patio. More screams. More panic. Someone yelled: *"He's got a gun!"* Dean peered over his shoulder. Demir stepped forward, aimed again. This time right at his head.

On instinct, Dean turned away, again trying to protect April with his whole body. He would not let her get this far only to be taken down now. Even if it meant having his own body riddled with bullets. Even if it meant his life. She was everything to him. He'd known that deep down from the first time he'd met her. He'd known it every moment of every day since he'd pushed her away last year.

But he didn't hear a second thud or take another bullet. Instead, he felt warm liquid splatter across the side of his face. At first, he feared it might be April. But she was alert beneath him and seemed okay. Dean whipped back around, watched as Demir fell limp to his knees, then crumpled sideways onto the patio. That was when Dean noticed the giant hole in the killer's head, and when he realized that the warm liquid on his face was the assassin's blood. Someone else had shot him. Who? Where? He searched and thought he recognized someone in the distance. Eric? Was it his brother?

More screams suddenly filled the air from the other partygoers. Mad panic had set in. People scurried everywhere. The music dramatically stopped onstage. People began knocking each other down, women tripping over high heels, men shoving other men out of the way. It was every person for themself in a mad dash for safety. Dean's shoulder throbbed and he was beginning to feel weak. But he knew he couldn't stay still. They had to get out of there. Dean pushed himself up on wobbly feet, lifted April from the concrete, and they rushed to escape in a pack of others.

FIFTY-FIVE

"We need to get you to the hospital!" April exclaimed.

They were a block away from the hotel. People in fancy dresses and tuxedos were still running in all directions up and down the sidewalks. Sirens were echoing throughout all of downtown, the first police cars to arrive jumping curbs and flooding the entrance to the JW Marriott. Dean's mind was swirling. He had come face-to-face with an international assassin and survived. But his left arm felt numb, and blood was dripping all the way down his sleeve and off his fingers. Still, he felt okay. A little lightheaded. But okay. He wasn't thinking about the hospital at the moment. He was thinking about April. If he hadn't tucked his shoulder in front of her, she might be dead right now. The bullet was headed for her. He had allowed her to talk him into staying for the duration of this ordeal, but April had to leave town. Now. Before someone else took another shot at her.

"April, you need to go to the airport right now. Get on a plane. Get out of town. Go someplace where nobody can find you."

She seemed surprised. "Why? I can help you. You're hurt, Dean. You're bleeding badly. We need to get you to a doctor. And then get your story written. I can corroborate everything for you. Make your story more credible."

It was true. But he didn't care. "Look, I'll be fine. I'm not going to the hospital yet. I'm going to the newsroom. But you're not going with me. The feds will be knocking on my door soon. Hell, they might grab me at any moment. They'll want me. But they may also want you. If that happens, we're right back to the conversation we had a few days ago about them asking you to testify."

"Don't you think they'll have enough to pursue justice without me?"

"Maybe. But I don't really want to take that chance at this very moment. Not with dangerous people still out there."

"But they'll use you to get to me, Dean. They'll threaten you with jail time like your brother did earlier. I don't want to put you in that situation."

"That's why you can't tell me where you're going. Get off the grid, use cash, avoid contact with anyone."

She bit her bottom lip. "For how long?"

"Until you feel safe."

She stared at him, swallowed. Right then, Dean knew with certainty what he was feeling for April was being reciprocated. He reached over, took her hand, and squeezed it. He let go when he spotted a cab dropping someone off on the corner in front of them. He grabbed April by the elbow, rushed in front of another couple, got to the open door before them. More sirens were blaring behind them. Ambulances and fire trucks were racing down Second Street. Crowds were forming at every corner, people huddled, gawking, wondering what the hell was going on at the JW Marriott. A war was going on inside of Dean, and he knew if he didn't put April into a taxi in the next thirty seconds, he would change his mind. And that would put her at risk. So he practically pushed her into the back seat, yelled at the driver, "Get her to the airport as fast as possible!"

He turned back to April, who seemed frozen in the moment. There was nothing else to say. No words. Nothing that felt appropriate. Nothing that would make this less difficult. When would he see her again? Weeks? Months? Ever? He shut the door, banged on the top of the car to get the driver moving. His eyes remained locked on April in the back seat until the cab sped down the city street. Dean turned, looked behind him at the chaos that had formed around the hotel. Police cars were everywhere. He could even hear helicopters already hovering overhead. Dean touched his shoulder again, grimaced. It was starting to hurt like hell. But he was only two blocks from his office building. He stumbled down the sidewalk and hoped he wouldn't bleed out.

FIFTY-SIX

They gathered in the main conference room.

Dean stood at the window, observed the hotel in the distance. There was a swarm of red and blue flashing lights. News helicopters were swirling in the sky. He touched his cheek. He'd washed the blood off his face in the restroom, but he could still feel it on his skin. Remnants of the assassin's blood and tissue remained on his shirt. His arm was in a sling. A medic had been called in by Harvey. The medic said, on first inspection, he didn't see any nerve damage. Looked like the bullet only got muscle tissue and somehow made it out cleanly through the other side. It was going to hurt like mad for a while, but Dean would live. But the medic insisted that Dean go to the hospital to get it checked out more thoroughly as soon as possible.

Standing there at the window, just thirty minutes after nearly getting slaughtered by an international assassin, Dean could only think about April. He prayed she was okay. He checked his watch. He would find no peace until he thought she might be in the air to somewhere safe. He had no idea where she would go. And that twisted his gut.

He turned to the room, regarded Harvey and Fred and several other editors spread around the table. They were devouring the eight-by-ten photographs from the mailbox, haggling over what should go on the front page of the website. The tension in the room was palpable. They were also reviewing a rough outline of the story Dean and Harvey had been working on together the past few days.

Harvey walked over, handed him a cup of coffee.

"How're you doing?"

"I'm worried."

"I'm sure she's fine. She's very resourceful. Doc said the shoulder is going to be okay?"

"Yes, I'll live."

Harvey looked out the window. "Quite the ruckus over there."

"Tell me about it."

He patted Dean on his good shoulder. "Son, how does it feel to come face-to-face with a famous assassin and walk away?"

"I can't feel a thing right now."

"Well, you'd better start feeling something. I need someone to finish up this story."

"You write it."

They shared a fleeting smile.

Harvey shook his head. "No, sir. This is your baby."

All eyes seemed to finish reading the outline around the same time. For a moment, they all looked up, stared at each other with stunned faces.

Susan Halston, another editor, was the first to speak. "This is beautiful."

"Outstanding," echoed Bernard Jackson, a metro reporter, normally a pessimist.

These sentiments were shared throughout the room.

Fred Morley, the publisher, a large man with gray hair, turned to Dean. "Where is the girl, Dean?"

"She's gone, sir."

"For good?"

"For now."

"Did Hossle Jester really say this?" Fred asked, tapping the paper with a finger.

"Yes, sir," Dean replied. "Every last word of it. There were dozens of witnesses."

Fred rubbed his chin, shook his head, let it all settle. Then he stood at the head of the table, leaned forward on both heavy palms. "Okay, folks, we've got a lot of work to do. A lot of quick background-checking and verifying. But can anyone see any reason not to run this story tonight?"

Harvey was the first to respond, with a resounding: "Run this sucker."

The others immediately chimed in.

"Print this baby."

"Run it!"

Dean typed furiously with one hand while Harvey looked over his shoulder. He felt ridiculous, but Harvey insisted he do it, even one-handed. Harvey said he'd remember this moment for the rest of his career. They were a good team. His editor read from a notepad he'd personally filled up throughout the day. Dean started with Hossle Jester and the gulf oil-spill disaster, with hundreds of billions of dollars on the line, and then shifted to Senator Lambert's position of influence as head of the Senate investigation committee. He alluded to the blackmail story that broke earlier in the day that further tied Lambert to Hossle Jester and gave them a unified motive. Then he shifted to the evidence his father had left behind that tied all relevant parties together in a stunning way. From there, they tied in Andrew Rainer, Senator Lambert's chief of staff, whom they could not reach for comment, along with the legendary assassin, Yusuf Demir, whom they were trying like mad to confirm was the man lying in a puddle of blood a quarter mile away from them. He left out his father faking his own death and committing fraud. He had no idea if he'd ever see his dad again, but he still wanted to protect him as much as possible.

April was never mentioned. There was no need for it. She was simply a source. Dean had collected most of the information while they'd worked in tandem. Harvey didn't argue. It was an explosive story. The main conference room was turned into the war room. The editors argued over bold headlines and pictures. This was their online publication's only chance to be the center of the news world, and no one wanted to squander the opportunity. Fred introduced Dean to Reese Harris, *TexasNow*'s lead attorney. Fred wanted the attorney to review the story and make sure there were no legitimate legal ramifications that might come back to bite them. He also wanted Harris to brief Dean about his situation and obligations with the FBI.

Dean huddled by the window again. He checked the airlines on his phone. A lot of flights had left town over the last couple of hours. He wondered which flight she was on. He said a prayer for her safety while also praying his story might provide the protection April needed to come back to him as soon as possible.

FIFTY-SEVEN

Eric and the FBI finally arrived.

Dean watched over his computer screen as Eric made a dramatic appearance in the newsroom, followed closely by six other imposing agents. All heads stopped and turned. Everyone knew his brother's face. A chaotic bullpen suddenly went very quiet. Fred Morley stepped out of the conference room with Reese Harris beside him. Dean would go alone. He'd already discussed this with Harvey and the attorney. He would be fine.

Harvey whispered over Dean's shoulder, "Big brother is here."

"Surprised it took him this long."

"You sure you don't want our lawyer with you?"

"I'm good."

Dean stood as Eric approached. "Hey, bro. Your car or mine?"

"Let's go, Dean."

Minutes later, they were back in the same office suite where Dean had met with his brother earlier. Eric poured himself a cup of coffee. Dean accepted a cup. It was awful coffee. But he was glad to have something. His mouth was parched. The curtains were closed. Dean had counted at least a dozen agents in the other rooms around the suite.

With his back turned, Eric said, "You're very lucky to be alive, man."

"Do I have you to thank for that?"

"Yes. Be glad I'm still a good shot."

"I'm very glad. How did you know I was there?"

"I'm good at my job. You thought you were being cute with your little boat excursion. But I'd already tagged you with a GPS device in this building."

Dean hadn't even thought of that. He was thankful for it now.

"Can you verify it was Yusuf Demir?" Dean asked.

"This is my interview, Dean."

"Right. Well, I owe you."

Dean pulled a copy of his news story out of his jacket pocket, handed it to Eric.

"What is this?"

"Hopefully my get-out-of-jail-free card."

Eric set his coffee down, unfolded the story, and began reading. Finished, he set the paperwork down in front of him. His brother's whole demeanor changed. It was as if someone had pumped life back into him.

"You've verified all of this?" Eric asked. "And you're going to publish it?"

"Yep. With a big, bold headline. After getting your comments on record."

"There are some things in here I can verify, if you fully cooperate."

Dean smiled. "I'll do my best."

"Was that April with you tonight?"

Dean's smile disappeared. "Where?"

Eric stared at him. "Don't play games. I saw her. And Ben told me she came to talk to him at the bar the other day. She's involved with all of this?"

"No, she's not. Leave her alone."

"You think I can't find her, Dean?"

"You have enough to do. Please."

"Between you and me, I'll do my best. But I can't guarantee the demands my bosses will make on me as this all unfolds."

"Fair enough."

"You said Dad was connected to all of this. But there is no mention of him in your story."

"I was mistaken."

Eric eyed him carefully. Dean didn't want his brother to know the full truth about his dad. At least, not yet. It would only put Eric in an impossible situation as a federal agent. He wanted to protect both his dad and his older brother. If their dad was still alive, they would address the matter when they found him. If he was dead, there would be no reason to ever bring it up. But this would only work if Eric let it go. For a moment, Dean wasn't sure his brother would do that. The look on his face told Dean his brother wanted to push the conversation. His job was to investigate. But he was holding back.

Finally, Eric said, "Okay. Good to know."

Dean knew that meant his brother understood the situation.

"Is he still alive, like you said?" Eric asked.

"As of three days ago. He's been living in Costa Rica. Can you get people there to search for him?"

"I will as soon as I walk out of this room."

Dean sighed. He was exhausted. "Can I go home now?"

Eric grinned, shook his head. "Sorry, bro. You're going to be stuck with me for a while. We've got a lot to talk about. Better get comfortable."

"Terrific."

FIFTY-EIGHT

Hossle Jester sat in the forward cabin of his private plane that evening. The jet was a Gulfstream G550 that would fit up to sixteen passengers. But Jester rarely traveled with anyone else on the plane other than his flight staff. The seats were made from the best Italian leather. Everything sparkled and shone appropriately. The plane had the latest technology, with a huge flat-screen TV on one wall. Jester had purchased the plane two years ago from ExxonMobil for $38 million. He held a glass of scotch and watched the TV while continuing to peek out the window at the tarmac. His pilot had popped his head in a few minutes ago and said they were working on runway clearance. Should only be a few more minutes.

Jester tapped his fingers on the leather armrest. A local news channel was on the flat screen. Video footage was rolling from the JW Marriott. TV reporters were trying to uncover exactly what went down, but no one really knew much. At least one man was dead. They knew that. They were unsure about much else but were working hard to get the details. Jester touched a button and flipped to another channel. It was also showing footage from the JW Marriott. Thankfully, there was no mention of his name yet.

Jester touched the glass to his lips. Inside, he was still fuming. Yusuf Demir had been instructed to take out the reporter and the lawyer earlier in the day when it became clear they were a real threat. Jester's private security contractors in DC had confirmed that. But the assassin had allowed them to get within a few feet of Jester. How was that possible when he was paying the assassin more than $40 million? If Demir hadn't been shot dead already at the hotel, Jester would've been looking for another assassin right now to take him out. He was that angry about it.

Jester thought about his exchange with the reporter. His temper had gotten the best of him. He could still see the smirk on that reporter's face before he walked away. Jester wondered what they knew. Surely it was mostly a bluff. There was no way he could have pieced so much together so quickly. Still, he'd called Edward Sullivan, his attorney, in the limo on the way to the airport, and instructed him to destroy anything that might connect them back to Lambert. Shred every single piece of paper he could find. And destroy the firm's computer servers immediately. Hell, burn down the whole damn building. He'd build them a new one. He also ordered his attorney to get out of town. Get out of the country.

The Gulfstream started to creep forward. Jester grinned, relaxed.

Once in the air, they'd never find him. He had homes all over the world. A man can hide for a very long time with a billion dollars in the bank. He was bigger than that news reporter. Bigger than the feds. Bigger than Senator Lambert.

A female attendant walked up, asked him if he needed anything else before takeoff. He rudely waved her away without a word. The plane turned onto a runway with lights, eased forward, started to pick up steam. Jester dropped his head back into the cushions. He'd survived much worse than this mess. He heard the jet engines engage, closed his eyes. His breathing was easier. Then suddenly the jet engines powered down and the plane began to slow. Jester opened his eyes, peered out the window. That was when he saw them and felt the air go out of his lungs. A dozen red and blue lights blinking in the dark night, racing down the runway toward the plane.

FIFTY-NINE

Edward Sullivan exited the elevator of his office building and stepped into the parking garage underneath. His heart was racing. He had three paralegals and two secretaries in his massive office right now with four shredding machines, destroying anything and everything he could think to destroy. And then more. He didn't care if they were legitimate client files. It didn't matter anymore. Nothing mattered but getting away from all this. An IT guy was also supposed to be in his office right now, wiping out his entire computer system. The staff seemed confused but didn't argue. They did whatever he told them to do. He was the godfather of the firm.

But he could not wait around anymore. A bomb had gone off in the city, and the roaches were scrambling for the corners. He had to leave the country, and fast. Before they somehow tracked him down. He would fly to the islands first. Hide out there for a while, just like Jerry Dawson, his old friend and partner who'd betrayed him so callously. Maybe Jerry had been right all along. They should have both gotten out of this situation while they could. They already had millions. But the allure and promise of hundreds of millions was too much to pass up.

Sullivan had the second reserved parking spot. When he stepped around the corner toward his Mercedes, he froze in place as fear shot through him from head to toe. Four muscular men covered in tattoos were waiting for him. These were not Americans; he could tell. They were angry Mexicans. And Sullivan knew right away they were from the Zeta Cartel. He had not wired them the full transfer of funds. He cursed under his breath. The men spotted him and stepped forward. Sullivan had nowhere to go. He could run, but they would be on him within twenty strides. He was done. He knew this was not going to be pretty. He'd heard stories where these guys had chopped off hands and feet, torn off lips, ripped off ears, used acid and blades, and every vile way of taking a man's spirit and life. Right now, he'd give anything for a revolver and one bullet so he could do it himself.

As they reached him, strong hands gripping his arms and legs, he began to beg and plead for his life with the promise of millions. They could have everything. The trunk of his Mercedes was opened, and he was dropped inside into the pitch-dark a moment later.

Alone, Sullivan began to weep like a baby.

SIXTY

Andrew Rainer sat on the battered carpet in a cheap motel outside Bethesda, where he'd been hiding since news broke on Senator Lambert's assassination earlier that morning. There were pills spilled on the carpet beside him, empty bottles of beer scattered throughout the room. The ugly red curtains were pulled tightly shut. He'd thrown his cell phone into a lake on the drive over. Rainer hadn't stopped shaking all day. If they would kill a sitting senator, they would have no problem killing a lowly chief of staff like him. He would be next. He just knew it. They were dealing with a crazy man. Rainer had thought of turning himself in to the feds. But that would just lead to prison. He was a dead man either way. He was either going to prison for a very long time, if someone didn't choke him in his first few days, or an assassin was going to put a bullet in the back of his head when he was sitting around watching Jimmy Fallon one night.

There was no way out. His life was over.

Just four days ago, he and Senator Lambert were talking about another run at the White House in four years. Things were looking up. With Carson out of the way, they could again rally the troops. They could really do it this time. They could win the whole damn thing. They believed it. Rainer had pictured himself sitting in the Oval Office, right next to the most powerful man in the world. But everything had crumbled down on top of them. His fearless leader and mentor was dead. Brutally killed in his own home. And now he was sitting on the floor in a dirty motel, waiting to die. Waiting for a man to crash open that cheap wooden door and put bullets in his head.

Rainer glanced over to the bed. The black revolver sat there staring back at him. It had belonged to his father. They'd used it for target practice out by the pond near their farmhouse when he was growing up. His dad would put out empty soda cans, and Rainer would pick them off one at a time. His mom had given him the gun when his dad had passed away from cancer three years ago.

Hearing footsteps outside the door sent chills through him. He tensed up, held his breath, waited. Then they passed without incident. It had been like this all day. Rainer couldn't take it anymore. His nerves were shot. He popped another two pills in his mouth, found a bottle, drank them down.

His world was spinning. He pushed himself up, stumbled over to the bed.

Just do it. Don't even think about it. Just do it for them. Save them the time.

He picked up the revolver, placed it in his mouth, pulled the trigger.

SIXTY-ONE

The vehicle screeched to a halt. A door was opened. Jerry Dawson was blinded but felt strong hands suddenly on his shoulders. The person helped him up and guided him outside of the vehicle until his bare feet touched dirt. When the person let go, Jerry immediately fell to the ground. His legs were so weak. His mouth was parched. His head had been pounding for days. But he was at least out of that hellhole. Where was he now? What was happening? Around ten minutes ago, two men had barged in to grab him in the tiny, barren room he'd been held captive in for the past week; at least, he thought it was a week. It had been difficult keeping track of time because he'd been in and out of consciousness throughout. They'd blindfolded him, wrapped duct tape around his hands and feet, and then dragged him away and put him into the vehicle. He thought it might be a van from the way it had bumped so roughly down whatever streets they'd been traveling.

Jerry felt his hands and then his feet cut free of the duct tape. Seconds later, he heard the vehicle rumble and take off. Jerry slowly lifted the blindfold from his eyes. It was nighttime. He'd been unsure of it at first. His tiny room had no windows. Day and night had meant nothing to him for a long time. He turned, his neck aching, watched as the old white van disappeared down a dirt road. His blurry eyes slowly came into focus, and he began scanning the area. There was what looked like an auto shop across the dirt road. Several cars were stacked outside, tires missing, hoods up. He saw two guys with their shirts off working under the hood of a truck. Jerry looked down at his hands and feet. Was he actually free? Had he just been released? Was this real?

He heard a male voice behind him.

"¿Está bien, señor?"

Jerry pivoted. He spotted a young man wearing blue scrubs approaching. Behind him, Jerry noted a white building with the word *médico* in the title. Was it a hospital? When he didn't respond right away, the guy repeated himself in English.

"Are you okay, sir?"

"No, I need help."

"I can see that. Let me get a gurney and get you inside."

The medic hurried back inside the building and then returned with two other hospital workers and a gurney. They helped lift Jerry onto the carrier and then pushed him toward the doors of the hospital. Jerry again stared down the dirt road. The van was gone. So were the guys inside it. Was it over? The questioning, the beatings, the torture, the agony? To his recollection, he had never revealed the location of the blackmail photographs on Hossle Jester's boat and the communication between Edward Sullivan, Senator Lambert, and Jester about hiring Yusuf Demir. He also never told them about Trisha. So why had they let him go?

Inside the building, a team of medics began examining him. With each step of their care, Jerry began to breathe easier. He had survived. He was still alive. There had been a point when he'd given up hope. If he had been let go, he wondered what was happening back in the States. Had everything unraveled? Was Trisha okay? He began asking for a cell phone. The staff assured him they would get him one just as soon as they assessed his injuries and made him more comfortable. They shot him up with pain relievers. Jerry didn't fight them. He began to feel good for the first time in what felt like forever.

SIXTY-TWO

April sat in a quiet airplane thirty thousand feet above the earth.

The plane was half full. All the seats had TVs in the backs of the headrests. At first, she didn't bother watching. But then she noticed a woman across the aisle getting ready to watch an FBI news conference, so April turned on her TV and put on the headphones. Eric Dawson was on the screen. She couldn't believe the words as they came out of his mouth. Yusuf Demir had been shot and pronounced dead. They had arrested Hossle Jester, the man they believed to be the mastermind behind the assassination of Carson and Lambert. Hossle Jester had not acted alone. This was a conspiracy involving the highest levels of government. Eric went on to describe all the connecting components.

There was no mention of her. And no reports about a dead journalist. Her biggest fear over the past couple of hours was that Dean would not survive his gunshot wound.

For a split second, April felt happy. Dean was going to have his moment. He had worked so hard. They had worked so well together. And they'd just pulled off one of the biggest stories in years and brought evil men to justice. But then reality hit her hard. She was in a plane on the way to nowhere, unsure where she was going, how long she was going to stay, and what she was going to do next. That felt scary.

Worst of all, Dean was not sitting beside her.

She turned off the TV. She couldn't handle any more tonight.

For now, she had to shut off the emotions.

She just had to survive.

SIXTY-THREE

A rookie FBI agent dropped him off a few minutes after midnight.

Dean stood on the sidewalk outside his apartment. He was so tired, he wasn't sure he could even climb the stairs. So he turned around and just sat on the bottom step. He stared up into the clear sky. A brilliant moon shone down on him. His neighborhood street was very quiet. A few tree branches swayed as a cool breeze pushed through.

Eric told him he thought Dean would be safe on the streets. He said his team was reporting that the bad guys were running for cover. They'd already apprehended a couple of high-priced private security contractors who'd been hired by Jester. Word had gotten out that the dam was busted and the game was over. Nevertheless, Eric suggested he still be extra careful for a few days. Dean didn't want to watch his back anymore. He didn't want to notice suspicious looks. But he knew he'd be doing that for some time. It had become second nature. He wanted to say a final goodbye to Oscar and Felix, to his other pursuers, and certainly to any assassins. It was over. They'd done it.

But April was gone.

Dean ran a hand through his hair, grimaced as pain shot through his shoulder. He hated the way April had had to leave. A rushed goodbye that lacked the proper words. He wanted to call her, tell her how much he missed her already. He wanted to wrap his arms around her, hold her tightly. He wanted to protect her, to love her, but he could do none of that right now, and it caused tears to well up in his eyes. He wasn't sure what to do next. His whole life had been consumed by helping April, and now it was finished. Sure, it was a thrill to publish the story. But he felt a strange emptiness inside. Relieved and sad at the same time. There would be more stories to write for weeks, months, but all that just seemed tiresome to him right now. In this moment, he'd rather be somewhere else. He'd rather be getting lost with a beautiful and brilliant woman.

Headlights approached. Dean felt a jolt of fear until he recognized Harvey's Jeep Cherokee. His editor parked at the curb, got out, approached with what looked like a six-pack of cold beer.

"Hey, champ," he said, looking tired himself. "Beer?"

"Sure," Dean said, smiling.

Harvey popped open a bottle, handed it to Dean. He took a big gulp, cradled the bottle in the fingers of his free hand.

"So what do you think?" Harvey asked. "You see our home page?"

"It's a good page."

Harvey grinned. "Yeah. Pretty good." He sipped his own beer. "A man could retire on a story like this one."

"Who are you kidding, Harvey? We'll be taking you straight from your office to the morgue one day."

"You're probably right. This is too much fun." His editor finished off his bottle. "You ever heard of the Pulitzer, Dean?"

"Whatever."

"We've already fielded over fifty calls from big media outlets around the country with people wanting to talk to you. You're the man of the moment."

Dean rolled his eyes. He'd been so focused on protecting April and getting justice for all the deaths, he'd never given any thought to what might happen with his career when his story went public. The Pulitzer was so far from his mind. And the thought of talking to the media felt nauseating. Right now, he didn't care.

"So where do I go from here, Harvey?"

Harvey looked over, laughed. "You miss her that much already?"

"So much it hurts."

His editor nodded, stared at the sky. "You remember my city council story?"

"You and Janice?"

"Then you know how the story ends."

"I hope you're right, boss. Because any other alternative feels devastating."

"Give it time. Give her time."

"Time is all I have now."

SIXTY-FOUR

Three weeks later

The ski boat whizzed across the waters of Lake Travis. Dean held on tight to the railing. He watched his two nephews in the water behind the boat, grabbing on to a tube attached by a rope for dear life, the biggest smiles he'd ever seen on their faces. Dean's father sat behind the wheel of the boat, sunglasses on his face, tan and trim, looking happier than he'd ever seen him. His father was still recovering from his brutal captivity. The story he'd told was awful. But he also accepted responsibility for his role in all of it and wouldn't stop apologizing. He was stupid, and it had hurt his own family again. Dean was still struggling to reconcile his father's selfish actions. After all, his choices had left a wake of destruction that led to Sally Kimble's tragic death and had almost gotten April killed. But his father seemed deeply remorseful and swore he would financially take care of Sally's children. Dean knew it was going to take some time to get over what his father had done. But at least they had the time.

Trisha Sullivan had returned home to Austin to bury her husband. Dean knew she had also privately reunited with his father. They were planning to build a new life together when enough time had passed.

Eric and Tina sat close together in the front of the boat, looking like they were ready to end the marital strife between them. Eric said they were a work in progress, but he was happy to have moved back into his house again. Ben and Jenna sat across from him. They had scheduled their wedding day for two weeks after they both graduated. Ben had even asked both Dean and Eric to be his co–best men. Dean's help bringing his father back from the dead had quashed all the tension in their relationship. He was glad. They were all an imperfect family again—somehow closer than they'd ever been.

Dean's father whipped the boat and pushed forward on the accelerator. The boys could barely hang on as the tube hit a wave and sent them sailing into the air. Everyone laughed. They all seemed happy. But something was missing for Dean. April. He'd spent the better part of the past three weeks drowning himself in his work, all in the hope of not having to think about how much he desperately missed her. At first, it was easier. Life was a circus. There were stories after stories. But she still dominated every spare thought. He constantly wondered about her. Where was she? Was she okay? Did she keep up with all the breaking news? Was she missing him at all? Most important, why had she not reached out to him? She was safe. She would not have to testify. She could come home and reclaim her life. Start over with him. But he was beginning to worry she didn't want that, after all. That fear was keeping him up at night.

Dean pulled out his phone when it buzzed. His eyes narrowed. It was a text message from a random phone number. He didn't recognize the area code. It was a photo of a small cabin in the woods in front of a beautiful snowcapped mountain. He could see a physical address listed on an exterior mailbox. The capturing of the address looked intentional. There were no people in the photo. But there were three words typed directly below it. They were three of the most beautiful words he'd ever read.

I miss you.

Dean carefully drove the rental SUV down the mountain road.

He finally came to a stop in front of a small, isolated cabin home. Dean put the car into park, took a moment to soak in the majestic surroundings. He peered out the window. There were mountain peaks poking up all around him, pine trees stretching forever without interruption. He hadn't seen another house for the past half mile. His eyes drifted over to the cabin. He checked the address again. This was the place. His knees felt a bit wobbly as he got out. He was nervous. He wore blue jeans, an untucked flannel shirt, and hiking boots. He had one bag. He wasn't sure how long he'd be staying. He wasn't sure if he was staying at all. He wasn't sure of much. Only that he had to come. He stood beside the rental car, breathed in the crisp, clean mountain air. He could hear the crackling of a brook off to his right.

Dean took a few steps forward toward the cabin.

The front door opened.

And then she was standing on the porch in front of him.

He lost his breath. His heart was pounding. She wore a white sweater and blue jeans. Her hair was different. Shorter, a shade darker. But she was as beautiful as ever. They both just stood there a moment, staring at each other. He swallowed the knot in his throat. Then she glided down the steps and threw her arms around him. Her lips moved to his, and they kissed. It was one to remember. He pulled her in close, absorbed her smell, her touch. It was a dream. One he'd had countless times while sitting on his balcony, staring at the city and crying into his beer over the past three weeks.

But now the dream was real.

She took a half step back. "I didn't know if you'd come."

"I couldn't get on a plane fast enough."

"I thought maybe you'd forgotten about me."

He smiled. "Believe me, April, I tried. Harder than I've ever tried to do anything in my whole life."

"It didn't work?"

"Nope."

She returned the smile. "Good."

They kissed again. They held hands, moved up the steps. He got the grand tour of the place, a vacation rental, and then they had lunch together on the back porch. Afterward, they sat close together on a wooden swing. Dean marveled at the mountain landscape. It was heaven. With April snuggled up under his arm, he did not think life could get much better.

"Have you kept up with everything?" he asked.

"Of course. I read every single story. I printed them all out and sort of made a scrapbook. I know that's goofy, but I missed you. I wanted to stay connected to you. I thought you were going to work yourself to death."

"I tried."

She snuggled up even closer. "It's over. Right, Dean?"

"Yes. It's over. The coast is clear."

"I can finally come home?"

"Yes, please. I don't want to live another moment without you."

"Good. Because my bags are already packed."

They kissed again.

He never wanted to stop.

ABOUT THE AUTHOR

Photo © 2019 Amy Melsa

Chad Zunker is the Amazon Charts bestselling author of *Not Our Daughter*, *The Wife You Know*, *All He Has Left*, and *Family Money*; the David Adams series, including *An Equal Justice*, which was nominated for the 2020 Harper Lee Prize for Legal Fiction, *An Unequal Defense*, and *Runaway Justice*; and *The Tracker*, *Shadow Shepherd*, and *Hunt the Lion* in the Sam Callahan series. Chad studied journalism at the University of Texas, where he was also on the football team. He has worked for some of the country's most powerful law firms and has also invented baby products that are sold all over the world. He lives in Austin with his wife, Katie, and their three daughters, and is hard at work on his next novel. For more information, visit www.chadzunker.com.